MOONLIGHT MAYHEM
By
Helen Haught Fanick

Moon Mystery Series, Book II

To Chris –
Best wishes!
Helen

For Liz and Dave

ACKNOWLEDGMENTS

My family includes several writers, and I'm grateful to all of them for their endless love, support, and encouragement. My gratitude also goes to those who have read my work in manuscript form and suggested corrections and changes. Included are Ben Rehder, Ed Fanick, and Vernon and Marguerite Shettle. Books have always been important to me, and I can thank my family for this, too—the parents and aunts who read to me when I was young, and those who always made sure there were books in the house. And to Becky Rehder, my gratitude for designing superb book covers.

CHAPTER ONE

Grandma Flynn believed in living life according to the signs of the moon, and she taught my sister Andrea and me everything she knew. Andrea, being a natural skeptic, never believed a word of Grandma Flynn's wisdom, but I've always been sure she was right. The dark of the moon is a time of trouble. The waning halfmoon means turmoil and disaster, and the waxing halfmoon means change, but sometimes a positive change can occur in that phase. The twenty-four hours surrounding the full moon are when good luck flourishes; we experience harmony, peace, and good fortune. That's why it's so hard to understand what happened on the night of the full moon, that last Saturday in June, the night of the wedding.

Ivy McGee and I talked my niece Maggie into getting married that particular Saturday evening rather than some other date in June. Ivy works at the Alpenhof Hotel in West Virginia's Canaan Valley, and Maggie works there, too. In addition to that, Maggie's engaged to the owner of the hotel, Stefan Novacek. Ivy believes in living by the signs of the moon, just as I do, so when Maggie told us in January that she and Stefan were getting married the following June, we immediately checked the calendar and found there was a full moon on the last Saturday of that month. It seemed like the perfect time for a wedding.

Andrea and I live in the little town of Pine Summit, and we drove to the Canaan Valley a couple of days early in order to help Ivy and Maggie get ready for the wedding, which would be held under a large sugar maple on the side lawn of the hotel. Asbury McGee rode with us—he's Ivy's husband—since he's a native of Pine Summit and had hitchhiked to his brother's house to pick up some things he'd left there.

Asbury sat behind us with the sun turning his fringe of silver hair into what looked like a halo that had collapsed around his head. "I think Maggie and Stefan are gonna make a fine couple," he said as soon as we got started. "Ever since the ski season ended, they've been working together like a couple of beavers to remodel the attic and add some more rooms up there. She works right along with him, and they done made a lot of progress."

"Are any of the rooms in the attic ready for guests?" Andrea asked.

She was thinking what I was thinking, that the hotel would be full of wedding guests. Well, our room was reserved well in advance, and I made sure it was our favorite—on the corner, at the back of the hotel, east wing. We had the room when we were there in the winter, and it provides a lovely view of the valley sweeping away toward the mountains, and out the back window, we could see the beautiful woods. I was hoping that area would be full of rhododendron bushes in bloom.

"Stefan put some rollaway beds in the attic for some of their ski school friends who'll be coming," Asbury said. "The two lower floors should fill up if everyone shows up that made a reservation. There's more than enough room for all the relatives on the two lower floors."

Andrea pulled into a McDonalds at a crossroads. "How about some breakfast?"

"I'm ready," I said.

We sat down with our Egg McMuffins and coffee, which Asbury insisted on paying for. In spite of his rough upbringing, he has an inherent chivalry which isn't that uncommon in our Appalachian Mountains. I'm not sure how much he makes as a handyman at the Alpenhof, but he wouldn't listen to our objections, so we let him pay.

"Are preparations for the wedding already underway?" Andrea asked.

"Ivy and the new hired girl been busy cleaning up all the rooms. Giving them a good going-over, they are. Everybody's been real busy, what with the kids working in the attic, too. Now and then we get an interruption from that woman named Eva that lives down the road."

"Is she still there?" I asked. "I'd have thought she'd be back in Germany by now."

"Oh, she's still there. They're saying her husband and her are getting a divorce. If you ask me, she's way too flirty with

2

Stefan, and him about to be married. I hope she don't cause trouble at the wedding."

We met Eva Weiss when we stayed at the hotel in January, and we were very much aware at the time that she was making a desperate play for Stefan. Her husband had returned to Germany, and we heard rumors even then that he was getting a divorce. Bad as I hate to, I have to admit the woman's a true beauty, with her long blonde hair and ice-blue eyes. And I'd never admit it aloud, but she truly outshines Maggie in that area. Maggie's the girl next door, with her short auburn curls and a few freckles across her nose. Pretty, yes, but not a great beauty. The news that Eva was still in the valley cast a shadow on my previously sunny mood. I decided it was time to change the subject.

"Had any of Stefan's relatives arrived from Europe before you left for Pine Summit?" I asked. Andrea thinks mingling with foreigners is a broadening experience for us—me, I'm just nosy about what Stefan's relatives are like, and I freely admit it. After, all, they will be Maggie's in-laws.

"Nobody had arrived yet, but I think Stefan's parents were supposed to come the next day after I left."

"Stefan told me when we were here before that she's German, and his father's Czech. I wonder what they'll be like," I said.

"Not too hoity-toity, I hope," Asbury said.

Andrea smiled. "They'll be fine, I'm sure. Look how nice Stefan is." Andrea is totally comfortable with anyone and in any situation. She's a retired math teacher, a spinster, and she's always been brimming with self-confidence since the day she was born. She struck out on her own right out of high school and worked her way through the university. As soon as she had her degree, she began teaching at Pine Summit High School, where she taught math for forty years.

I, on the other hand, am a widow. My husband, John, died two years ago, leaving me fairly well-off. I miss him, but I'm content with my memories. I quilt with a group of my friends—we're all members of the Trinity Methodist Church—and I go to lunch frequently with one or another of them at our local Nell Flanagan's Restaurant.

When we went to the Alpenhof in January, Asbury was riding with us then, too, and he helped us find our way. This time, Andrea didn't need any help. That's Andrea. Her sense of direction is unerring, so I always let her drive. She scares me, whizzing around our mountain roads in her Honda Accord, but she always gets us there.

We pulled into the Alpenhof parking lot about four in the afternoon. I was surprised to see they had painted the place. When we first saw the hotel in January, It wasn't what I had expected. I had imagined a sleek but rustic chalet with a huge stone fireplace in the lobby. Instead, we saw a boxy rectangle, a three-story frame structure, painted white, with porches on the two lower floors. The third floor was the attic I mentioned earlier, the one the kids are converting into additional rooms.

Now the building was painted a deep brown, with window boxes full of geraniums at all the windows. "I like it," I said, and Asbury beamed.

"Stefan and me did it," he said. "We had some help from David, too, once school let out for the summer. He helped us finish up." David is Ivy's fourteen-year-old son from a previous marriage.

"It looks much better," Andrea said.

We got out as Andrea popped the trunk, and Asbury insisted on carrying our bags and coming back afterward for his three plastic grocery sacks full of possessions. I wondered what was in those bags; if it were clothes, Ivy would undoubtedly give them to some local charity the minute he took them from the bag. Asbury's life has improved considerably since he married Ivy; he wears clothes that are clean and new-looking now, and Andrea and I are happy about the change.

He took our suitcases from the trunk, and Andrea and I got our cosmetic cases. "They put you in Room 10 again, just like you asked," Asbury said.

As we approached the hotel, I could see four Adirondack chairs and some tables on the porch. I had a pleasant mental image of sitting there with an early-morning cup of coffee. On the second floor, I was able to see more chairs and tables through the railing. This was another change that made the place look inviting. We walked into the lobby, which is located in the middle of the building, and saw that it had been painted, too. It was a soft spring green, perfect for the woodsy surroundings. Ivy was behind the registration desk, and she came out and hugged us. "I'm so glad you're here. Maggie and Stefan went to Parsons to see about the flowers for the wedding, but they'll be back shortly. Thanks for giving Asbury a ride."

"We enjoyed his company," Andrea said. She filled out a registration card and also signed on a large registration book which lay open on the counter. I signed, too, thinking as I had in January that this must be an old world custom, the registration book. I couldn't resist the impulse to look at the other names on the page. Three had signed in yesterday— Franz Novacek, Erika Novacek, and Laszlo Novacek. Franz and Erika were Stefan's parents, but I hadn't a clue who Laszlo was. Stefan's an only child. An uncle, maybe?

We went to our room, and I plopped down on one of the twin-size beds. "Did you notice the signatures on the registration book?"

"Yes, I noticed."

"I wonder who Laszlo Novacek is."

"He's Stefan's uncle."

Andrea amazes me. I'm the nosy one, but she's always the first to know everything. "How did you know that?"

"Maggie told me on the phone the other day that Stefan's Uncle Laszlo was coming. He's Franz's brother, of course. I called her to see how wedding preparations were going, thinking we could come earlier than we'd planned if we were needed."

I decided I'd better get up off the bed and get organized. "We're going to be here a while, so why don't we unpack and put everything in the chest and closet? Our suitcases will fit under the beds."

"Good idea," Andrea said. She immediately began putting things in the two lower drawers of the chest. She's four years older than I am, but I have to confess she's in better shape, so I was glad she'd be the one doing the bending. While I'm quilting or watching TV, she's out hiking around Pine Summit, which is built on a hill.

Our room was small, but we had adjusted to that idea when we were here during the winter. There was no phone or TV— just a four-drawer chest between two side windows, two twin beds, and a nightstand with a lamp between the beds. The hotel had once been a boarding house for the loggers who cut West Virginia's red spruce, and I imagined at that time there had been one bathroom per floor. Somewhere along the way, changes were made, rooms were sacrificed, and now each room has a bath.

I finished unpacking, putting the plastic-bagged dress I'd wear for the wedding in the closet with a few other things. I went to the side window and looked out over the valley. Then from the back, looking into the wooded area, I could see the rhododendron bushes were blooming under the trees. In January, two feet of snow had covered the ground, and the pine branches were so loaded they sagged to the ground. "It's just as beautiful in summer as it was last winter. Everything's so green."

Andrea joined me. "It's lovely. Makes me want to find a trail and go hiking."

"Makes me want to find a bench under a tree and read a book."

"I guess what we need to do is check with Ivy and see if there's something we can do to help get ready for the wedding."

We went to the lobby, where Ivy was talking on the phone. On the east side of the lobby, a brick fireplace stands against the wall. Facing the front of the hotel, two newly-upholstered chairs flank the fireplace. Opposite them, a couch covered in the same dark green fabric stands. A round coffee table sits between. A tall man who was dressed in jeans and a tweed jacket was seated on one of the chairs, and he looked up as we came in. It was impossible not to notice that, even though he looked to be in his sixties, he was incredibly attractive. He had green eyes like Stefan's and dark hair with just enough unruly curl to give him a roguish appearance.

We approached the couch to wait for Ivy to finish on the phone, and he gave us a smile that indicated he was delighted to meet not just one, but two women. "Ladies," he said, as he got up with a little nod and shook hands with both of us.

6

"We're Maggie's aunts," Andrea said. "I'm Andrea Flynn, and this is my sister, Kathleen Williamson."

"I'm Laszlo Novacek, Stefan's uncle."

He shook hands with both of us, and we all sat down. "Did you just arrive?"

"We got here at four. I understand Stefan's parents are here, too."

"They're out exploring somewhere. They'll be back later, and we're planning to go to the lodge for dinner. Would you care to join us?"

The Alpenhof has no restaurant, so we usually go to the lodge at the Canaan Valley Resort for meals. I was getting hungry already, and hoped it wouldn't be too long before the party got on the road.

Before I could say anything, Andrea said, "We'd like that." She looked at me to make sure I agreed.

"Fine," I murmured. It would be a chance to get to know Stefan's family. "We're in Number 10. Would you knock on our door when everyone's ready to go?"

"Certainly. You can ride with me. I have a rental car. Stefan and Maggie can go with Franz and Erika."

I wasn't so sure I wanted to ride with the suave Laszlo Novacek. In spite of his good looks, or maybe because of them, he was a mite too suave for me. I didn't want to rock the boat, however, so I didn't say anything. Ivy was finished with her phone conversation, so we excused ourselves and went to the desk. "Is there something we can do to help you get ready for the wedding?" Andrea asked.

"Not at the moment. I don't know if Maggie told you, but they hired a new woman to clean rooms when they promoted me to handle the desk. Her name is Hadley Ferguson, and she's a part-time student at Davis and Elkins. Maggie and me pitched in and helped her, and we gave all the rooms a good cleaning. Got everything spic and span for the wedding guests."

"There's nothing to do in the kitchen?" I asked.

"No, we went through and washed everything and even scrubbed the cabinets while we were at it. We don't have enough china and glasses for the wedding supper—we'll use paper and plastic—but we washed what we have in case some

7

folks want to have breakfast here, or in case it's rainy at night. You remember how we used to have soup and sandwiches when we were snowbound. We do the same if it's raining hard."

"Do we know yet how many guests will be here?" Andrea asked.

"It's not going to be a big wedding. I think they invited fifty at most, and you know how it goes—probably thirty will show up."

"I suppose they invited everyone from the ski school, since Stefan and Maggie both work there, but I imagine a lot of the instructors have gone elsewhere for the summer," Andrea said.

"Some are working at the lodge and at restaurants around the valley, I hear. Then Maggie said some college friends of hers will be coming."

"Thank goodness, since Andrea and I are Maggie's only relatives," I said. "She'll have some folks on her side of the aisle."

Andrea nodded. "That will help. But what about chairs for the ceremony?"

"Stefan came up with a bunch of folding chairs from somewhere. They're all stored in the kitchen right now, but of course they'll be moved outside for the wedding. We'll be serving the food in the kitchen after the ceremony, so the men will bring the chairs back in for the reception."

We stressed the idea that we were available to help with whatever was needed and then retreated to our room, where I hoped to take a short nap. Andrea put on her hiking boots and said she'd be back in time for supper.

#

I'd been dozing for what seemed like seconds when there was a knock at the door. Andrea wasn't back yet, or maybe she was. "Are you in the bathroom?" No answer. I staggered to my feet and went to the door, expecting to see the charming Laszlo, but it was Maggie instead.

She hugged me, then held me at arms length. "I'm so excited! I'm so glad you're here." She squeezed me again. She was in jeans and a WVU tee shirt, and her auburn curls looked a bit windblown.

It was wonderful seeing her so happy. "Did you see Andrea?"

"She was on her way out when we got here. She said she was going for a short walk. She'll be back in time to go to dinner. She said you were napping, so I waited till the last minute to come and see you."

"We met Laszlo. He invited us to ride with him to the lodge."

Maggie laughed. "Better watch it! He's a womanizer of the highest order."

"At his age! He must be at least as old as we are. Is he married?"

"He's older than you are. Seventy, I think. And he's never been married. Never could decide which one of his women to settle down with, I hear. He should be coming down shortly to gather you and Andrea up for the ride to the lodge. Stefan's upstairs changing. We're supposed to ride with his folks."

"You say Laszlo will be coming down. He's in an upstairs room?"

Maggie giggled. "We put him up there where we could keep an eye on him. He's across the wide hall from Stefan, the one that leads back from the staircase to the back of the hotel, and he's across the west wing hall from my room. He'll have a hard time making any moves, at least until we leave for the honeymoon. After that, you're all on your own."

I felt somewhat reassured that Maggie still had her own room. Of course, that didn't mean she was sleeping in it. Maybe she was just using it as a dressing room for the wedding. Oh, well, they'd be married soon. That would take care of sleeping arrangements. Andrea and I had met her in Charleston and helped her pick out a gown, which she said she'd take home and hang in her room.

"So when will you leave on the honeymoon?"

"We have a reservation at the Marriott in Charleston Saturday night, after the wedding. We'll leave from there Sunday morning."

"Still not telling anyone where you're going?"

She smiled and looked dreamy. "Not a word. No cell phones, no laptops, just two weeks of blissful peace and quiet away from the hotel. We've been working too hard, and I can't tell you how much we're looking forward to this break."

"Have you had a lot of guests since ski season ended?"

"We've had lots. We're booked up on weekends, practically through the summer. It's so much cooler here than it is in D. C., that we're a really desirable destination. Some folks come for a week or two of vacation."

"Ivy and Asbury are very competent. I'm sure they can handle things while you're gone. We'll be here for a few days after the wedding, and we could stay for the full two weeks if you'd like."

"That won't be necessary. We gave them your phone number, and Andrea's, in case of emergency. I think they can handle anything that comes up, though. This old hotel is basically very sound, and the plumbing and electrical were updated before Stefan took over. There won't be any problems."

We heard another knock at the door. "That must be Laszlo. What time is it?"

"It's seven." Maggie opened the door.

Laszlo stood there in a jacket and tie, looking spiffy. He was no longer wearing jeans; instead, he'd put on a good-looking pair of slacks. Here I was in my polyester pants and shirt that I'd worn for the trip to the hotel, and planned to wear out to eat. "Andrea went for a walk, and she isn't back yet."

"She's waiting for us in the lobby. Let's go on to the lodge, and the others will join us there."

I gathered up my purse as Maggie scurried out the door to go upstairs and change. We collected Andrea, still wearing her hiking boots and jeans and looking great in spite of that, and went out the front door. Laszlo escorted us to a big, black Cadillac at the edge of the parking area. I headed for the backseat, and he opened doors for us. I settled into what I thought must be leather. Of course, I've never gotten acquainted with leather car seats, so I'm not positive they were leather. Whatever, I was impressed.

We waited in the lobby of the lodge for only a few minutes until the others showed up. We were introduced to Franz and Erika, and all congenially insisted on first names. After all, we were going to be relatives of sorts. Franz was also in a jacket, but with no tie. He looked a lot like his brother, but lacked the charming scoundrel aura that Laszlo exuded. Erika looked neat and trim in a brown suit that was probably silk, with a scarf tied just so at the neck. She had short blonde curls and blue eyes that radiated intelligence and friendliness.

As usual, I was feeling the inadequacy of my polyester wardrobe. I knew Andrea was having no such misgivings about what she was wearing. As I said before, she's brimming with self confidence, and in addition, she's one of those people who look elegant, no matter what she puts on.

The seven of us sat down at a table for eight, and Laszlo made a point of squeezing into a chair between Andrea and me. I was across the table from Erika, a spot I liked for finding out more about the family.

I ordered the London broil, something from the mid-range-priced items on the menu, in case there was a hullabaloo over who would pay for what and Andrea and I ended up being guests of someone else. Andrea ordered the vegetable strudel. Finally, all the orders were taken, and we settled down to chat about the wedding, about everyone's travels to the valley, and about who else might be coming.

"It seems that Maggie and Stefan have things well in control," Erika said.

"Yes, I'm proud of them. They know what they want and seem to have it all organized," I said. "We asked Ivy if there was anything we could do to help, but she said most everything's taken care of. Of course, when it comes time to prepare the food, we'll help her in the kitchen."

"Is Ivy the lady at the desk?"

"Yes. She does a good job there, and her husband, Asbury, is most useful as a handyman."

"I must tell her that I'd be delighted to help also. I'll just plan on being in the kitchen Saturday to do whatever is needed. But where is the kitchen?"

"From the lobby, you go through the alcove where the ice machine's located and the kitchen is just beyond. There's a laundry room off that alcove, too, if you need to wash clothes."

By this time I had decided Erika was going to make a good mother-in-law for Maggie. She seemed bright and cheerful, which was half the game. As for Franz, he hadn't said much, but now he looked at Stefan and said, "Did Agnes and Claudia let you know they're coming?"

Everyone glanced at Laszlo in what I thought was a rather intriguing manner, and then back at Stefan, who said, "Yes, Claudia emailed me. They're arriving in Charleston tomorrow and will rent a car. They should be here before evening."

Stefan looked at Andrea and me, realizing we were being left out of the conversation. "Agnes was my nanny when I was a kid. She's a lovely person. Claudia's her sister. I was surprised they agreed to come, but I'm delighted they did."

He said this with such emphasis that I couldn't help wondering just what complication involved Agnes and Claudia. Erika, bright smile on her face, changed the subject. "You must tell me about your little town of Pine Summit. Maggie tells me she was born there. It sounds very much like the little town where I grew up, in Bavaria."

Andrea spoke up from the other side of Laszlo. "Pine Summit's a very small town. I think we had five thousand residents at last count. The town started as a farm on top of a hill. The owners named the place Pine Summit, and then the town grew up all around, and down to the river. It's a hilly area, and great for hiking. The original farm is now a city park, and it has a hiking trail. It's a pleasant place to live."

"It sounds heavenly. I miss the small towns. We live in London now, but as Stefan has probably told you, we've lived all over. It always seems to be big cities, of course, since Franz is with the diplomatic corps."

That cinched it. Erika was okay in my book if she liked small towns. I couldn't help wondering about Franz, though, because he was so reserved. Could he be a spy? Then I gave an inward chuckle. My imagination tends to run wild when meeting the intriguing foreign types who come from Europe or the Eastern Seaboard and frequent the Canaan Valley. Franz definitely seemed to be an intriguing foreign type.

By this time we had finished eating, declined dessert, and the men were hassling over the bill. Andrea and I tried to protest, saying we'd pay our own and wanted to pay for the kids, too, but Franz and Laszlo wouldn't hear of it. Laszlo had his credit card out first, and that settled it. Franz demanded to be allowed to pay next evening, when it was assumed by the Novacek clan we'd all be eating together again.

Maggie headed for the rest room, and I followed her, hoping we'd be the only ones in there. She was already in a stall, and we were alone. I stood next to the door and whispered. "I'm curious. What's the big mystery about Stefan's nanny and her sister?"

"Is there anyone else out there?"

"No, we're alone."

"Stefan hasn't told me too much about the situation, but he did say that Laszlo was engaged to Agnes at one time. That was years ago, of course. Turned out he had an affair with Claudia while engaged to Agnes, and that's when it hit the fan."

I wished Maggie wouldn't say things like that, but at least she hadn't used the s--- word.

She went on, "The engagement was broken, and the sisters were estranged for years, but they finally made up and apparently started blaming Laszlo for the episode, as if he were the only one responsible."

"Good grief. I guess what you said was right. Someone needs to keep an eye on him."

"He's seventy now and has heart problems. I hope he's settled down some. Anyway, he came on the same plane with Franz and Erika and will be leaving with them, so they'll be here all the time he's here."

"I wonder why he rented a car, and they did, too. Seems like they all would have come together."

"I suppose they thought they might want to do different things. I guess you enjoyed the Cadillac."

"It's luxurious. Did he rent that car in Charleston?"

Maggie had come out of the stall by this time. "He probably arranged to have it delivered there if it wasn't available in Charleston. Apparently, when Laszlo wants something, he can make it happen."

"It sounds like he has money."

She was washing her hands. "Bunches. He's a wheeler-dealer from the word go. He's lost plenty at times, but manages to recover, according to Stefan."

"I wonder who he'll leave all that money to." I was fishing, as usual, and hoping it would be Stefan.

"We don't know. Maybe a home for ageing Casanovas."

By this time Maggie was drying her hands, and we walked out together, laughing. *Finally*, I thought, *I found out some things before Andrea*. I'd tell her when we got to our room tonight.

CHAPTER TWO

It was after eight o'clock when I woke up Friday morning. Andrea had left the room, as usual, and was probably drinking coffee with Ivy. I got dressed and went to the lobby, where I found them both sitting in front of the fireplace with their cups. The fire someone had started last night had gone out, and no one had bothered to start another. It was supposed to be in the seventies later in the day.

"Have some coffee," Ivy said, motioning toward the kitchen with her cup.

I helped myself and came back to sit down with them.

"Ivy says there's nothing to be done toward the wedding right now, so I asked her to go to breakfast with us over at Blackwater, but Asbury's gone to bring in a load of wood, and she can't leave the desk."

"Won't be anybody checking in but wedding guests, but I'll have to be here for them. I can't leave. I haven't been to the Blackwater Lodge in years, so maybe sometime after the wedding we can go."

"We'll plan on it," I said. "We're going to stay a few days afterward. It's nice up here in the summer. It was so cold in January, I nearly froze."

We finished our coffee and got ready to go to the lodge at nearby Blackwater Falls State Park, one of our favorite places. "Do you suppose we'll see Willard there?" I asked. Willard Hill is a deputy with the Tucker County Sheriff's Department. We met him when we were here during the winter, and he always seemed to show up when food was being served. He was our best source of information about what was happening in the valley, so we always hoped we'd run into him.

We like to walk down and see the falls when we go to the park. Or I should say, Andrea likes to walk down and see the falls. I love to see the falls, but I don't enjoy the walk, especially coming back up the stairs. Andrea takes pity on me, and we always rest on a landing. I insist on going down before eating, because climbing those stairs on a full stomach would be too much for me. And hiking down and back before breakfast is a great sacrifice, because I'm usually famished by the time we get to the park.

We made it down the stairs and were surprised to find Willard Hill at the bottom platform, gazing at the falls as if in a trance. *Willard must be in love again*, I thought, remembering his unrequited love during our last trip. Otherwise, why wouldn't he be in the restaurant inhaling biscuits rather than looking so dreamily at the falls?

"Hello, Willard!" we both said as we approached.

For an instant, it seemed he didn't recognize us. Then a wide grin spread across his face. "Miss Flynn! And Mrs. . . . ."

"Williamson. So good to see you, Willard. And we're Andrea and Kathleen, remember? We persuaded you to use our first names when we were here before."

"Okay, Andrea and Kathleen. How are you?"

"We're fine," Andrea said. "Here for the wedding, of course. You'll be there, won't you?"

His face lit up. "I wouldn't miss it! I was just standing here thinking that this would be a great place for a small wedding."

Somehow, I thought more was going on with Willard than we knew at the moment. "And the sheriff? Will he be there, too?"

"Yes, he's coming. We're all hoping for a quiet Saturday night, so most of us can be there."

I had high hopes in January for a budding romance between Sheriff Ward Sterling and Andrea. He's a most attractive man—tall, well-built, about our age, a widower, and what's more, just as quiet and thoughtful as Andrea. I always wonder if Andrea is lonely, never having married and living alone. Of course, I live alone, too, but I have my memories of John all around to keep me company. The sheriff did come to Pine Summit for a weekend in April and took both of us out to eat at the Courthouse Cafe in Martindale, our county seat, and I think he and Andrea email each other, but theirs hasn't been the hottest romance in history.

Andrea pulled out her digital camera, one of her many gadgets, and started taking photos of the falls. "I'll get one of the three of us in front of the falls." She set the camera on a railing and set some buttons, then moved to the other side of Willard. She showed us the picture and promised to email a copy to Willard.

"Let's go eat!" I said, and we began the long ascent to the parking area. We stopped at the landing, as usual, and I was huffing and puffing while the other two were hardly winded at all. *I really must start getting more exercise*, I thought.

At the restaurant, the hostess escorted us to a table beside a window. From there we could look out toward Blackwater Canyon. Andrea and I ordered bacon and eggs, and Willard said he'd have his usual two biscuits and coffee. I couldn't help wondering whether he had breakfast at home and then a biscuit break later. He's skinny as a rail, but some people stay that way, no matter what they eat.

"So what's happening in the valley?" I asked when the waitress left us.

Willard looked thoughtful, and I could tell he was going to work up to important news gradually. "Birdie Lancaster's making the wedding cake, did Maggie tell you that?"

We met Birdie in January. We had gone to her house to get some information about the Alpenhof, since she had worked there when she was young. At one time, it was known as the Valley Hotel and had been owned for a brief time by our grandparents. Birdie served excellent coffee and luscious chocolate chip cookies while telling us everything she knew about the history of the hotel. How can you forget a visit like that?

The waitress brought coffee, and we added half and half. "Maggie mentioned that Birdie's making the cake," Andrea said. "I'm sure it'll be wonderful, if it's as good as her chocolate chip cookies."

"She's one of the best cooks in the valley," Willard said. "One of Maggie's friends from the ski school is working for the summer at a florist in Parsons, and they're doing the flowers."

"It's nice when people you know are involved," I said.

"Otherwise, I think that's about it. Well there is one other bit of news. Have you met the new lady who's working at the Alpenhof?"

Here comes the biggie, I thought. "No, we haven't met anyone new there. Just saw Ivy and Asbury."

"When they promoted Ivy to work at the desk, they hired this other woman to clean. She's a part-time student in criminology at Davis and Elkins."

"Yes, Ivy mentioned her. Hadley, I think her name is."

"Yes. Hadley Ferguson." Willard suddenly had that dreamy look again.

Andrea set down her cup. "I'm sure we'll meet her soon. Does she work every day?"

"Yes, she's taking morning classes, so she's there every afternoon. They've been really busy on weekends, so she has to work then."

I assumed Willard is in his mid-thirties and has never been married, according to Ivy. "Who'd have him?" she said once after he'd stopped by the hotel and helped himself to two of the Danish pastries we were having for breakfast. Anyway, I couldn't help wondering whether he would be much older than Hadley, and just what their relationship was.

I couldn't resist asking, "So, are you and Hadley seeing each other?"

Andrea gave me a quick scowl, but I ignored her. She doesn't always appreciate my nosiness, and I suppose that's because she always seems to know everything without asking.

"Our schedules make it tough, but we've been seeing each other for a few months now. I did take Hadley to a movie last week. And we've gone hiking at Blackwater Falls a few times with her son."

So Hadley has a son. Maybe she would be age-appropriate for Willard, after all. I wondered what sort of step-father he'd make. Maybe he'd be okay with kids. But then I was thinking far away down the road, as usual. "How old is her son?"

"He's seven. They live with her mother, and she looks after him while Hadley's at work and school, or if she's not there, her maid does." I wondered for a fleeting moment about someone in the Canaan Valley having a maid, but Willard had finished his biscuits and drank the last of his coffee, and he interrupted my thoughts with, "I've enjoyed the visit, but I need to go. It's my day off, and I have about fifteen errands to do."

"It's been good seeing you, Willard," Andrea said. "We'll see you Saturday evening. Let's hope for a quiet evening so we can enjoy the wedding."

"It's the night of the full moon," I said. "That's a time of peace, happiness, and good fortune, according to our Grandmother Flynn." I said this to Willard and ignored Andrea's skeptical look.

Willard smiled. "That sounds just about perfect. I hope we can count on it."

"I looked up the data on the moon last week, just for you," Andrea said. "The moon is actually full that morning, but it won't be visible in the valley at the time of the wedding. Moonrise is at 9:11 p.m., and with all the mountains around, we may not see it for some time after that. There's still plenty of sunlight at seven, when the wedding's scheduled to start."

"I know, but it's still the evening of the full moon. That's important." I refused to believe there would be anything but happiness and good fortune on that last Saturday in June. Now I know just how wrong I was.

#

We browsed through some shops in Davis, not buying anything, so it was nearly noon by the time we got back to the hotel. Ivy was behind the desk, checking in what appeared to be a family. Andrea and I sat down on the chairs by the fireplace. "That must be Stefan's other uncle and his family," I whispered. "I can't remember his name."

"Becker. Klaus Becker. He's Erika's brother."

"I know. I guess that's all the relatives present and accounted for."

Klaus turned and said something to his wife in German. He was a paunchy man of medium height with thinning blonde hair. His wife was trim, with dark hair. I couldn't see her face, so couldn't tell more about her. The two girls with them were slender blondes, both looking like they were in their teens. They finished the registration process and headed for the wing of the hotel opposite ours without coming over and saying hello. But then I don't suppose they had any idea who we were.

"I guess we'll meet them when we all go to dinner tonight," I said. "Except for Maggie and Stefan's young friends who'll

19

be here for the wedding, I guess that just leaves Claudia and Agnes." I was still feeling a bit miffed, because when I started to explain about the sisters last night and their involvement with Laszlo, Andrea already knew about it. Maggie had given her a lot of detail about Stefan's family in an email. I'm out of the loop without a computer, or at least that's what Andrea tells me. And why didn't she tell me all she knew before we came to the valley? Sometimes I think she's wrapped up in her own little world most of the time, and it wouldn't occur to her to gossip about anyone.

I was sitting there thinking about the sisters and wondering how long it had been since they last saw Laszlo when two women walked in. I knew right away this had to be Agnes and Claudia. They were roughly our age, and they were the only older people still to come. They were a couple of sharp-looking ladies, both dressed in pant suits, and both with artistically-tied scarves around their necks. As usual, I wished I'd given more thought to what people would be wearing. Oh, well, my polyester pants and shirts and acrylic sweaters would have to do.

One of the sisters was pretty, with short, curly brown hair and a soft, vulnerable look. This must be Agnes, I decided, the one who had been engaged to Laszlo. She didn't look like she'd have an affair with a sister's fiancé. The other had sharper features, with short straight hair. She looked much more assertive, and she led the way to the registration desk. Like all the others we'd met so far, they spoke English with only a faint accent.

As soon as they had signed in, they came directly over to us, and the one I thought was Claudia put out her hand. "I'm Claudia Martin, a friend of the Novacek family. This is my sister, Agnes Schulz. We're here for the wedding."

Andrea took her hand. "I'm Andrea Flynn, and this is my sister, Kathleen Williamson. We're Maggie's aunts."

We shook hands with Agnes also, who murmured, "So nice to meet you."

At that moment, David, Ivy's son, came through from the back of the hotel. He was in jeans and a flannel shirt, and looked like he'd grown three inches since we saw him in

January. He smiled at us and said to the others, "Are you the guests that need help with your bags?"

"Yes. They're in the trunk of the car." Claudia handed him a key. "Let's go to our rooms, Agnes. I want to change as soon as he brings our bags."

"We'll see you later," I said. "I suppose we're all going to dinner together later."

Claudia and Agnes looked at each other and didn't say anything for a minute. Finally, Claudia said, "I'm sure we'll see you later."

They had just disappeared down the wing on our side of the hotel when David came in with their suitcases. I couldn't resist giving him a hug, even though he had his hands full of bags. He grinned. "Nice seeing you again. How've you been?"

"We're fine," I said, as Andrea gave him an awkward hug also. She's never been the demonstrative type. "You've grown a lot since we saw you last."

"Yes, ma'am. It's Mom's beans and cornbread. I'd better get these bags back."

"A real West Virginia kid," I said to Andrea, "growing up on beans and cornbread. Maybe Ivy will invite us over for a meal sometime while we're here." Ivy, Asbury, and David live in a small house behind the hotel.

"That would be a real treat."

"I guess the sisters are in our wing. Sounds like they have separate rooms. She said 'Let's go to our rooms,' plural. Wonder why they wouldn't share."

"No telling. Claudia's in the room beside us, and Agnes is across the hall from her. Franz and Erika are beside Agnes, across from us."

Leave it up to Andrea to know all this. "So that's all for our wing. The other side has more rooms, but I think the Beckers are somewhat younger, so they can be over there with any young folks who have rooms in that wing."

David came back through, stuffing dollar bills into his jeans. He waved and walked on. "Gotta go help Asbury finish unloading the wood."

"I think I'll drive over to the park and find a hiking trail," Andrea said. "Want to go with me?"

"No, thanks! I'm taking a nap. I want to be bright-eyed and bushy-tailed, ready to observe all the high drama at the restaurant tonight."

#

The Beckers were already in the lobby when we got there at seven. He introduced himself, Klaus, his wife Karla, and daughters Amalie and Nicole. Amalie was in her first year of college, Nicole still a high school student. Karla had the look of the perennially put-upon wife, but Klaus didn't look like the type to take advantage of anyone. Perhaps it was the daughters. Amalie, however, was reserved and polite. Nicole had the permanent pout of the petulant teenager. Sometimes I'm thankful I never had children, and this was one of those moments.

Franz and Erika came out of their room, and then Agnes and Claudia. They all had obviously met and greeted each other earlier in the day, as no one had much to say. Then Laszlo came down the stairs, looking like a sultan surveying his harem. Or is it sheiks who have harems? Whatever, he looked like one or the other. He nodded at the sisters and went to give Karla a hug and shake hands with Klaus. He made a big fuss over the girls, all in what I thought was German in spite of the fact that he's Czech.

Then in English, "Who wants to ride with me? Plenty of room in the Caddy." He was looking directly at the sisters with a devilish grin.

Claudia turned without saying anything and headed for the door, followed by Agnes. We all went outside, where Claudia and Agnes got into a car which was definitely not the "Caddy." Andrea invited Laszlo to ride with us, but he insisted we use his gas, so we climbed into his car again. It wasn't too much of a sacrifice, lounging in that backseat, I must admit.

Maggie and Stefan had been out doing errands and would join us at the lodge, so there would be thirteen of us—an unlucky number, as far as I'm concerned, but I didn't bother to mention this to Andrea. Sometimes I think she believes I'm a tad nutty, and she may be right, but Grandma Flynn's beliefs have always stuck with me.

Someone must have called ahead to the restaurant, because they had a table ready for us. I couldn't help noticing that the sisters sat as far from Laszlo as possible. For that matter, so did the Beckers. I wondered what was going on there. Laszlo sat at one end of the table, surrounded by Franz and Erika on one side and Maggie and Stefan on the other. It looked as if they had formed a barricade, but whether it was to protect him or to protect the others from him, I couldn't be sure.

Dinner went on and on, with the girls wanting dessert and everyone having coffee while the desserts were consumed. I sat beside Stefan on one side and Karla Becker on the other. I tried to conduct a conversation with her, off and on, without a lot of success. I did find out that they live in a suburb of Berlin, and that Klaus owns a business. I couldn't make out what she was saying when she explained what it was. Of all those present, she was the least fluent in English. I told her all about Pine Summit, and she nodded politely. I'm not sure she understood.

We got back to the hotel at ten, and the sisters and Beckers vanished instantly. Laszlo insisted the rest of us sit around the fireplace, which now had a blaze going, and share a bottle of wine. Stefan and Franz brought some folding chairs from the kitchen while Laszlo went to his room and came back with the wine. Andrea and I went to the kitchen and brought back water glasses, which would have to do, since the hotel had no wine glasses.

Neither Andrea nor I drink wine. We're both virtual teetotalers, and in addition, wine gives me a headache. I felt a need to be sociable with Stefan's family, though, and I'm sure Andrea did, too, so we both had some, insisting on only a small amount.

After Laszlo finished pouring, I couldn't resist picking up the bottle. The label said Gianni Brunelli Amor Constante. *What a laugh*, I thought, *that Laszlo would pick that particular wine, if the name means what I think.* Or maybe it meant he was constantly feeling amorous about any woman who was near. He probably chose it because it had a pleasant, fruity taste that appeals to women in general.

We chatted about the wedding and the beauty of the Canaan Valley, dancing around the subject of the others who had vanished so rapidly after dinner. Finally, the bottle was empty and I was ready for bed. We gathered up the glasses and took them to the kitchen, where Stefan and Maggie insisted on washing them, telling us goodnight with hugs.

"Did Maggie tell you anything about the relationship between the Beckers and Laszlo in that email she sent?" I asked when we got to our room.

"Only that their relationship was strained. The problem has to do with the fact that Klaus Becker invested in one of Laszlo's ventures, and it failed. I gather Klaus was practically bankrupt. They even lost the girls' college funds. Amalie's going to a small college near their home, but she wanted to go to Heidelberg University. Maggie wasn't gossiping when she sent me all this information, you understand. She just wanted us to understand the family dynamics."

If she wanted "us" to understand, why hadn't Andrea told me, I wondered. I let it pass without comment, however. Andrea's difficult to understand at times and not the most communicative person in the world.

It was after eleven by the time we both had our showers. I had put on my flannel nightgown, because it's chilly in the valley at night, and when we put out the lights I walked to the side window to look at the valley in the light of the almost-full moon. It took me a couple of minutes to realize that there were two people sitting at the picnic table which is located directly in front of our window. I stared, wondering who it could be.

"Come here and take a look."

Andrea was already in bed, but she got up and came to the window. "Beautiful out there, isn't it? Oh, I see what you mean. That's David, and . . ."

"Who's he with?"

"I think it's the Becker girl. The youngest one. Nicole."

"Good heavens! She's the pouty one that looks like she's mad at the world. She's sixteen and he's fourteen. We've got to save him!"

"There's nothing we can do tonight. A discreet word to Ivy tomorrow will be in order, though."

"It certainly didn't take them long to get acquainted," I said.

"Teenagers move fast these days."

We went to bed, trying not to imagine what might be going on outside our window.

Asbury was behind the desk when we got to the lobby, and Ivy was in the kitchen. She had put out cereal, milk, bananas, and Danish pastries. The big coffee pot signaled that it was ready to provide stimulation.

Erika sat at one of the tables having a bowl of cereal. "Good morning. This is a nice surprise, having breakfast in the hotel. How are you this morning?"

"I'm fine," I said, helping myself to coffee. I poured some Cheerios and milk and sat down by Erika. "Are you and Franz enjoying your room?"

"It's small, but charming. I'm enjoying having no phone and television. It's a refreshing change. When there's a TV in the room, we feel compelled to turn it on, regardless, and end up watching some mindless program instead of reading."

Andrea joined us, we all finished cereal, and I eyed the Danish. Would I look like a pig if I helped myself to one of those huge pastries? *Erika is so tiny, and of course Andrea's slim, too, but what the heck*, I thought, *we're traveling.* Then Erika surprised me by reaching for a pineapple-cream cheese before I had a chance. That settled it, and I took one, too.

Ivy had already started cutting up crudités to go with dip she said she'd made earlier, and as we finished eating, we joined her. I started on the carrots, Andrea took the broccoli, and Erika chopped cauliflower. Maggie came in shortly, yawning. "Am I expected to work on my wedding day?"

"We've got it covered," Ivy said. "We have some big spiral-sliced hams ready for the oven, potato salad, baked beans, a huge fruit salad, and these veggies and dip. The guys iced down a lot of different drinks in the ice chests yesterday, and they're probably expecting you to help them move chairs outside this afternoon."

"Yes, they are. You'd think the bride would be shown more respect, wouldn't you?" She sat down with a cup of coffee.

"You'd better have some breakfast," I said. It's going to be a long day."

"I will, as soon as I finish this coffee."

"Where's Stefan?"

"Upstairs, checking our to-do list. Everything's pretty well under control, I think. We decided not to do any more work in the attic till after the honeymoon."

We finished chopping the vegetables, and Ivy insisted there was nothing else to do. "Why don't the rest of you go sight-seeing? I can't go today, because Asbury will be helping set things up outside, and I'll have to handle the desk. I think all the family is here, but I'm sure several of the kids' friends will be checking in today."

After much discussion, it was revealed that Franz and Laszlo were going to go climbing at Seneca Rocks, and the Beckers wanted to take the girls on the lift at the ski area. "What I'd love to see is Cathedral State Park," Erika said. "I've been reading about it in a brochure I picked up at the lodge."

"We haven't been there in years," Andrea said. "I'd love it. I wonder if Agnes and Claudia would like to go with us."

"They told me last night they have appointments to have their hair and nails done, and they wanted to look around the shops in Davis."

Heavens! Hair and nails! Having them done had never occurred to me, and I felt like I would surely be letting Maggie down. Oh, well, they'd have to take me as is. Andrea always looks elegant, with her graying hair drawn back in a chignon, and in addition, she's tall and slim, while I tend to be pudgy if I don't watch it every minute.

We met back in the lobby; Andrea and I were wearing sneakers and Erika had on a neat little pair of hiking boots. We were soon underway in jackets and sweaters; it was still chilly outside. I had insisted on riding in the backseat, so I wouldn't have to get the full brunt of watching Andrea zip around the mountain roads. I leaned forward. "I'm surprised Laszlo would be rock climbing. I understand he has a heart problem."

Erika turned toward me. "Oh, he's in great shape. He hikes a lot, and even ran in a marathon a while back. I don't think he has a serious problem. As far as I know, he doesn't take any medication for it."

I couldn't think of any tactful way to pry into Laszlo's rumored transgressions, so I said, "We met Stefan when we were here in January, and we're very fond of him. I think he and Maggie will make a fine couple."

"I agree," Erika said. "We're fond of Maggie already and we're looking forward to having her as a daughter-in-law. She and Stefan have so much in common, with the skiing and hiking."

I settled back and listened while Andrea and Erika chatted about the scenery. We reached the park and were immediately overwhelmed by the giant hemlocks that flourish there, a remnant of the hemlock forests that once covered much of Appalachia. Andrea and Erika got out cameras right away, and we took off on the Cathedral Trail, and then made a quick right on the Giant Hemlock Trail.

We stopped for frequent photos of the three of us with the biggest of the trees, and they both showed me which button to push when I took photos of them. We intersected with the Cathedral Trail again and continued on various pathways through the park for a couple of hours. We finally found a bench to rest on for a moment.

"I can see why they call this Cathedral State Park," Erika said. "It's such a beautiful area, it reminds me of the time Laszlo and I spent a few days hiking in the Schwarzwald. The trees there also give the impression of being in a stately church."

Andrea smiled and nodded, as if she weren't at all curious about why Erika would be hiking with Laszlo, and for a few days, yet. I couldn't resist looking puzzled.

"I knew Laszlo before I met Franz," Erika said. "As a matter of fact, Laszlo introduced Franz and me."

I nodded just like Andrea had, but I was hoping for a much more thorough explanation of the triangle—who was in love with whom, and when and why. None came, and Erika got up and began taking more pictures.

"I'm starving with all this walking," she said. "I want to buy lunch for the two of you if you can suggest a place."

"No need to buy us lunch," Andrea said. "Can you make it back to Davis without starving? We could eat at the Sawmill Restaurant there. I ate there once when we were here in January."

"That would be fine."

I had a salad at the Sawmill, but Erika ate a huge plateful of food. I would have hated her for being so slim and being able to eat so much if she hadn't been so nice. We lingered over coffee—at least Erika didn't have dessert—then headed back to the Alpenhof.

When we reached the parking lot, we could see that Asbury, Stefan, Maggie and David were just finishing setting up chairs outside, and a dark green wrought-iron arch had been placed near the sugar maple and interlaced with flowers. More flowers flanked the arch. An isle between the chairs led directly to the arch. I could see the wedding was going to be a simple but lovely affair. I began feeling better about not having my hair and nails done.

I think everyone took a nap that afternoon; the hotel was quiet. When we woke up, the spicy fragrance of baking hams had seeped into our room. We dressed, not for the wedding, but in jeans. We stopped in the kitchen and found Ivy alone, so Andrea said, "We noticed David sitting on a picnic table bench outside our window last night. He was with someone, and I think it was the youngest Becker girl. We just thought you should know." Being a retired teacher, Andrea believes parents need to be informed about their children's activities, and I agree with her.

"What time was this?"

"It was a little after eleven."

"That certainly bears watching. I thought he was in bed, asleep. Thanks for letting me know."

"It smells wonderful in here," I said. "Is there anything we can do to help?"

"Everything's under control. Hadley helped me with the potato salad after she finished cleaning, so everything's done."

From there we went to Maggie's room. On our way, we went through a lobby full of young people, all dressed for the wedding and chatting up a storm. Two of Maggie's girlfriends were with her in her room, including her best friend from ski school, who was also her maid of honor. She introduced us.

Andrea gave Maggie the pearls she inherited from Aunt Libby a few years ago, and I gave Maggie the sapphire ring I inherited. These things took care of something old, something borrowed, and something blue. The wedding dress was new. Not everyone believes in following these old traditions, but why tempt fate? Taking care of all this and the fact that the full moon would be bestowing its blessing practically assured a wonderful marriage, as far as I was concerned.

We went downstairs and had just reached the lobby when a woman came sweeping through the door and up to the registration desk, where Asbury was taking over for Ivy. "I need a room for the night, please," she said.

"I'm afraid we don't have any vacancies, miss. There's a wedding here tonight and we're full up."

This woman, too, had an accent, and as we came closer I got a good look at her. It was hard to tell just how old she was, but she obviously was old enough that you could say she must have been beautiful when she was young. She was wearing jeans and teensy high heels, and she had something purple, I'd have to call it a cape, thrown around her shoulders.

"I've traveled so far to see Laszlo," she said. "I'm supposed to meet him here. Can't you please find something for me? Anything will do."

Asbury looked as if he didn't know what to do. "Well, there's the attic. But I don't know if . . ."

"Oh, anything would be fine. Please, I'd like to register."

Andrea had stepped up beside her by now. "The hotel owner has put several rollaway beds in the attic to accommodate some of the couple's young friends. I don't know if that would be suitable for you. The stairs to the attic are rather tricky."

The stranger turned a radiant smile on Andrea. "That sounds like fun. A slumber party, isn't that what you call it?"

Andrea turned to me. "Can you find Stefan and see if there are enough beds up there for one more?"

I went upstairs and pecked on Stefan's door, and he answered wearing a nifty-looking tuxedo, his tie dangling around his neck. "I hate to bother you with this, but there's a lady downstairs who is desperate for a room. She said she's traveled a long way to see Laszlo. Asbury told her the hotel was full, but she insisted he find a place for her. He mentioned the attic, and she was delighted, said it sounds like fun. But are there enough beds up there for everyone?"

"Did she give her name?"

"No, she hadn't gotten that far yet."

"There are more than enough beds up there, I'm sure. How old is this lady?"

"It's hard to say. I'd guess somewhere in her fifties."

"I can't imagine who she is or why she showed up here looking for Laszlo. Anyway, if she can make it up the attic stairs I suppose it's okay. Be sure and have David carry her luggage for her. You and Andrea can show her the way up there. Wait a minute. I'll get a flashlight you can give her, since there's no light in the stairway."

He went to a desk at the far end of the room and returned with a flashlight. I took it back downstairs, where the lady was looking at me expectantly. "He says there are enough beds, and he gave me a flashlight you can use in the stairwell. There's no light there, so you'll have to be careful."

She waved her hand dismissively. "It's no problem." She began filling out a registration card Asbury had placed on the desk.

"Can you get David to get her luggage?" I asked Asbury, and he got on the phone and asked David to come over.

When he arrived, she handed him a key. "It's the yellow Corvette at the edge of the parking lot. It's just one suitcase in the trunk."

David looked pleased to be holding a Corvette key in his hand, ready to open a Corvette trunk. He went out and returned with a small bag.

"I left the rest of my luggage at the hotel in Charleston," she said. "I'll be returning there, so it seemed simpler. Do you know if Laszlo's here now?"

"I don't believe he's come back from Seneca Rocks yet, miss."

We went to the laundry room and opened the door to the attic stairs. "No problem here," the woman said as she tripped up the stairs in her spike heels, followed by David.

"Just be careful when you come back down," Andrea said. "David can bring your suitcase when you're ready to check out."

"Thank you!" she called from the top of the stairs.

"Who in the world do you suppose she is?" I whispered.

"That's what I'm going to find out," Andrea said as she headed for the guest register with me trailing. When we reached the reception desk, "It's a little difficult to read her signature. It looks like Juliet Gorsky."

Andrea takes everything so literally. When I said "Who in the world do you suppose she is?" I was interested in a lot more than the mysterious lady's name.

#

David was in charge of the music, being young and technically inclined. He was sitting on a chair at the edge, with some sort of small sound system beside him. We sat down to strains of *O Promise Me. It's nice that the kids chose some traditional music*, I thought. Soon the other seats around us were filling up, and no one seemed to pay attention to which side they should sit on, which was nice, since Andrea and I are Maggie's only relatives.

Franz, Erika, and Laszlo were sitting near us, and I couldn't help noticing that the Beckers and the sisters sat on the other side, as far from Laszlo as possible. It came as no surprise that Juliet Gorsky was seated by Laszlo. She had on a different pair of shoes now, still spike heels, and a lovely summer dress that made me think she had been planning on attending an outdoor summer wedding when she came. Laszlo must have invited her to come for the wedding.

There was no moon, just as Andrea had predicted, and the sun was shining on our backs, warming us and keeping the chill of evening at bay. I always say there's nothing more cheerful than sunshine, so the fact that it was shining helped to make up for the absence of the moon.

Stefan came in and went to the front, looking handsome and elegant in his tuxedo, and Franz joined him. He would be the best man, and was wearing a tuxedo also. The man was born to dress elegantly, and the tuxedo he wore said "he owns me," and not "he rented me." I had a vision of him, James Bond-like, beside a roulette table in Monte Carlo.

Franz had been sitting between Laszlo and Erika, and I noticed that when he got up, Laszlo moved over to sit beside Erika and Juliet moved beside him. I was curious about what was going through Laszlo and Erika's minds. Were they wondering what would have happened if they had been standing before a minister years ago rather than Erika and Franz?

Everyone was there, it seemed. Asbury and Ivy were seated near us, since every guest was at the wedding, and they weren't needed in the hotel. I was sure the answering machine would be taking care of any calls. Another woman I assumed was Hadley Ferguson sat beside Ivy. She was a pretty blonde who looked somehow as if she'd be a good match for Willard. A purse sat on an empty seat beside her, and I imagined she was saving the chair for Willard.

Asbury and David were both wearing suits, and I couldn't help wondering where they got them. Somehow, Ivy had managed to get them both dressed up as she thought appropriate for Maggie's wedding. She was wearing a long-sleeved print dress of a lightweight summer fabric that almost hid how raw-boned she is.

Not far from where we were sitting, I noticed Eva Weiss. I was surprised Maggie would have agreed to invite her, considering how she flirted with Stefan last time we were here. I suppose she lives alone in the rented house just down the road from the hotel, since her husband left for Germany. I hoped she wasn't going to make trouble for Maggie—not that Maggie couldn't handle it, but who wants to have to handle a problem on the evening of their wedding?

Sheriff Ward Sterling, Deputy Willard Hill, and a few other deputies showed up at the last minute. The woman I assumed was Hadley Ferguson moved her purse, and Willard sat beside her. The sheriff said hello to us and sat down beside Andrea. I wondered whether watching the wedding would give them ideas.

The music changed to the *Wedding March*, and everyone stood up and turned to the back, where Maggie was starting down the aisle, accompanied by Asbury. Her father died three years ago, and she has no other male relatives, so we all thought it would be appropriate if Asbury walked her down the aisle. She's gotten quite attached to him since he started working at the Alpenhof. He looked as if he might pop the buttons on his shirt, he was so proud.

Andrea and I had helped Maggie into her wedding dress earlier, and we had seen her trying it on in the store, but we weren't prepared for how beautiful she looked. A friend had helped her with her auburn curls, and though short, they were swept back into an elegant style.

By the time the ceremony reached "Do you, Margaret Anne Flynn, take Stefan Laszlo Novacek to be your lawfully wedded husband?" I was too choked up to continue paying attention to what was being said. Andrea dabbed at her eyes with a lace-edged linen handkerchief; a nice touch for a wedding, while I had only a tissue. The sheriff just patted Andrea's hand and looked uncomfortable at having two tearful women on his hands.

We managed to compose ourselves when the ceremony ended and joined in the hugging and kissing of cheeks. I was in a group of people waiting to hug and congratulate Stefan when Eva Weiss rushed in ahead of everyone, threw her arms around his neck, and kissed him directly on the mouth. My mouth fell open. He pushed her away at arms length, and I heard him say, "That was inappropriate, Eva." She smiled coolly and said something to him I couldn't understand.

I'm sure Maggie saw the whole episode, and I couldn't help wondering what would happen if Eva approached Maggie to congratulate her—which she did immediately. I moved closer in order to hear what was going on. Maggie put her arms around Eva, kissed her on the cheek, and said, "We're so glad you could come, Eva." What class! Maggie inherited Andrea's self-confidence, which could never be shaken by the likes of Eva Weiss.

Several friends had taken pictures of the whole process, and were continuing to do so now. Gradually everyone migrated to the kitchen, and the men in the group folded chairs and took them along. Some of the women helped also, but of course that didn't include Eva. She was too busy clinging to Franz's arm and gazing at him as if she were hanging onto his every word.

Ivy had already laid out paper plates, fancy ones with wedding bells, and sturdy plastic ware. We helped bring the food to the table, and then stood at the end of the line along with Ivy, Asbury, and David. I saw Franz and Erika ahead of us, filling their plates. Shortly afterwards, Eva took her plate and rushed to a seat beside Erika before someone else could sit there. She was smiling and chatting as if Erika were her mother-in-law, and not Maggie's. The woman just wouldn't give up! After everyone finished eating and got up and began moving around, she greeted everyone in the family, with special attention to Laszlo. It was obvious he was happy with the attention from a woman as beautiful as Eva. Since she and Stefan went to school together, I suppose she knows the entire family.

Juliet Gorsky was left standing awkwardly to the side while Eva monopolized Laszlo, and I went to her. "Are you comfortable in the attic with Maggie's young friends?"

"It's fine. They've all made me feel very welcome."

I'm glad someone has, I thought. It certainly hadn't been Eva, who was still chatting with Laszlo.

Maggie and Stefan moved to the beautiful three-tiered cake Birdie Lancaster had made and began cutting. It looked delicious, and offered an opportunity to have dessert without having to feel guilty about it. It's practically mandatory to have a piece of wedding cake, I figured. To refuse would be bad manners, and probably bad luck, too. Birdie stood on the sidelines, beaming.

Everyone hung around afterward, visiting and taking more pictures. Laszlo, now with Juliet at his side, made the rounds, introducing her as "my friend." I thought I detected a chill in her reaction to being called a friend, but that may have been just my overactive imagination. So many folks approached us to chat about the wedding, however, that we didn't give much time or thought to Laszlo and Juliet.

Finally, Maggie and Stefan disappeared and came back, both dressed in good-looking suits, and carrying suitcases. It was after nine, but they would go to Charleston for a late check-in at the Marriott. We followed them to their car, where someone, probably Willard and his friends, had tied a string of cans to the bumper and painted "JUST MARRIED" on the rear window. They were traveling in Maggie's ancient Volvo, which she inherited from her father, rather than Stefan's truck, which Asbury would need for returning the chairs and getting firewood. They insisted that the Volvo was more dependable than anything else on the road today. I said a little prayer that this was so as they drove away.

Andrea and I, along with Erika, Claudia, and Agnes, helped Ivy clean up the kitchen and stow leftovers in the fridge. No one mentioned the sudden appearance at the hotel of Juliet Gorsky, and I managed to refrain from asking if anyone knew anything about her or whether she had been invited to the wedding.

Asbury, David, and Franz gathered up all the wedding presents and took them to Maggie's room, then returned the key to Andrea. Maggie had given it to her in case she wanted to use the computer.

By the time we got to bed, we were ready for sleep, the sleep of two aunts who were satisfied that their niece had taken part in a simple but beautiful ceremony which would lead to a happy marriage. We went to sleep readily, and didn't wake up till the sun was beaming through our windows and the sound of a scream was resounding through the hotel.

CHAPTER THREE

Andrea got up immediately, put on her robe, and marched out into the hall. I followed her, and when we got to the lobby, the pretty blonde woman, the one I assumed earlier was Hadley Ferguson, was rushing down the stairs from the second floor, a lamb's wool duster in her hand. "He's dead!" she sobbed. "The man upstairs—he's dead!" She stopped at the bottom and sat down on a step, looking as if she might faint. Ivy stood behind the desk, looking bewildered.

"It must be Laszlo," Andrea said. "He's the only man upstairs." She went up, two stairs at a time, and I followed, somewhat more slowly.

I heard a noise behind me and turned to see that it was the woman who came downstairs, the one who screamed. She was calmer now. When we got to the top, I said, "Are you Hadley?"

"Yes, I'm Hadley Ferguson. Some of the people upstairs checked out early, and I was cleaning, when I noticed the door to Room 12 standing open slightly. I decided Mr. Novacek had checked out, too, and went in to clean. I started over to strip the bed, and there he was. It was obvious he was dead. I'm afraid I reacted badly, screaming the way I did, but I was startled."

"Believe me, I understand. I probably would have screamed and fainted, too." We moved toward the door and went in, and Andrea was coming toward us.

"I'm going downstairs to get my cell phone and call the sheriff. There's nothing we can do here. Let's get out without touching anything."

"Could you tell what happened to him?" I asked.

"No, but he definitely is dead. No pulse, and his body's cold."

When we got down to the lobby, Franz and Erika were standing there in their bathrobes, looking around. "We heard a scream," Franz said.

"I'm sorry to tell you, but I'm afraid your brother's dead." Andrea said. "The maid found him this morning."

Erika turned pale and sat down on the couch by the fireplace. Franz started for the stairs. "It can't be. We were just hiking yesterday. He was perfectly fine."

"Please don't touch anything in the room," Andrea said. "I'm on my way to call the sheriff." She disappeared down the hall.

Erika looked at me. Tears were streaming down her face. "The sheriff? You don't think he . . ."

"A law enforcement officer must be called in the event of an unattended death," I said. I wasn't sure of my facts, but I looked at Hadley, the criminology student, and she nodded in agreement.

Andrea came back to the lobby. "Ward Sterling will be here in a minute. He's just down the road, checking out a stolen purse at the lodge."

Erika was wiping her eyes on the cuff of her robe. "This just can't be possible. He was always so full of life." She got up and started for their room.

She had been gone only a few seconds when Claudia came into the lobby. Unlike the rest of us, she was dressed. "I heard something. What's going on?"

Ivy headed for the kitchen, and I was sure she was going to make coffee. That was her remedy for any crisis, a good pot of coffee. I followed her to see if I could do something to help, while Andrea started explaining the situation to Claudia. We found six pastries, the huge Danish type, still in the refrigerator, and I cut these in quarters so that anyone who wanted some could have a bite with their coffee.

We went back to the lobby, and Andrea was missing. I thought she probably had gone to get dressed.

"Coffee will be ready in a minute," Ivy said.

"I'll get Agnes," Claudia said. "We were going to drive to Elkins for breakfast and shopping, but maybe we'd better wait till after the sheriff comes and goes." She looked miffed that breakfast and shopping would have to be postponed because of the death of someone she obviously hated.

Franz came back downstairs, looking grave. "We'll have coffee in a few minutes," I said, but he walked on past me and back toward their room.

Andrea came back wearing jeans and a flannel shirt, so I went back to our room to dress. When I got back, Andrea and the sisters had gone to the kitchen. Andrea was getting down a stack of cups from the shelf above the sink. "I'll take a cup to Ivy," I said, and put the Danish on the table. I put a triangle on a napkin, took the coffee, and went out to the desk. The sheriff had arrived, Ivy had directed him to Room 12, and he was going up the stairs. An unusual numbering system exists in the hotel, and probably has since its early days as a boarding house. Rooms one through ten are downstairs, and eleven through seventeen upstairs.

I was feeling light-headed, whether from hunger or the death of someone in the hotel, I don't know. The others had already started on coffee and a piece of Danish, and I helped myself.

"I suppose he had a heart attack," Claudia said between bites. "I think he had a history of overdoing it."

Overdoing what, I wondered. Claudia probably would have some ideas on that. The sheriff came in shortly and sat down with a cup of coffee. "Harvey Davis is up there now." He looked at Claudia and Agnes. "He's the local medical examiner. They'll be moving the body to his office momentarily. We're closing the room and putting up a yellow tape till we find out the cause of death."

Claudia smiled. "You don't think he was murdered, do you?"

I couldn't help thinking she was enjoying the thought, considering the sly smile on her face.

"There's no sign of violence, but we have to be sure."

Agnes, who rarely spoke, did now: "Is it okay if we go to Elkins?"

"You're not planning to check out, are you?"

Claudia looked annoyed. "No, we were planning to stay a few days and explore the area."

I wondered if she was annoyed with Agnes for speaking up or with the sheriff for asking about their plans. Sheriff Sterling answered her, "No problem at all with going to Elkins. Have a good trip."

The sisters finished their coffee and left us.

I got up for more coffee. "We haven't seen anything of the Beckers this morning. Surely the commotion would have awakened them."

"Maybe they left early for sight-seeing somewhere," Andrea said. "We haven't seen Juliet Gorsky, either. I suppose all the young people got up early this morning and left, but she may still be in the attic."

Andrea took her cup to the sink. "I'll see if there's anything we can do to help with the wedding debris." She left, and I assumed she was going to check with Ivy. Within minutes she was back. "Asbury and David are returning the chairs and arch, and unless there's anything left under the maple tree, there's nothing to do. Ivy said there's still a little food left, so we should plan on having supper here tonight. It needs to be eaten."

I had finished my coffee. "How about breakfast? I wonder if the Bear Paw's open this time of year."

"Only during ski season," the sheriff said. "The Hickory Dining Room has a good Sunday brunch buffet, but it doesn't start till eleven. I think they have breakfast earlier."

"Could you get away to join us?" Andrea asked.

"No, I had breakfast hours ago, and I'd better stick around. A couple of deputies are coming, and we need to go over Mr. Novacek's room."

Andrea and I went out to check the lawn around the huge sugar maple, and as we went through the lobby, Willard and another deputy were going up the stairs. Willard waved at us and kept going. We passed the picnic table, which is located outside our window, on the way to the tree.

"I intended to look out last night when I got up to go to the bathroom to see if David and Nicole were still hanging out, but I forgot," I said. "There's something under the bench."

Andrea walked over and picked it up. "It looks like a page torn out of an address book. It has an email address on it. David and Nicole were probably exchanging that information, and one of them dropped it. Harmless enough, it seems. I'll ask David if it belongs to him." She put it in her pocket.

The area around the tree was spotless; Asbury and David must have picked up anything left there, and I was glad. I was hungry in spite of all I ate last night and didn't want to fool around cleaning up. "Shall we go to the lodge for breakfast? I don't think I can wait till brunch."

"Let's get our purses and go."

Most of the breakfast crowd had left the Hickory Dining Room when we got there. However, the Beckers were sitting at a table by a window. "Maybe we should tell them about Laszlo," I said.

"Yes, they need to know."

We told the hostess we needed to speak to the others and went to their table. Klaus stood up. "Would you like to join us?"

I didn't know where we'd sit, since they were at a table for four, so I simply said, "Thanks, but we thought we should let you know that Laszlo was found dead in his room this morning. His body has been taken away to the medical examiner's office, and the sheriff and a couple of deputies are checking out his room."

Klaus's expression didn't change, but he relayed this information to the rest of the family in German. "Thank you for letting us know. We're just finishing, and must go on back to the hotel." The rest of the family didn't have any more of a reaction than Klaus did.

I couldn't help noticing that the girls were having a biscuit and milk, and Klaus and Karla had only coffee. I wondered whether they'd had breakfast earlier, and this was a snack after going for a hike. Or perhaps their finances were so stressed that this was their breakfast.

Andrea and I went to the table originally indicated by the hostess, and the Beckers finished their snack, or whatever it was, and left. "Did you notice what they were having?"

"I noticed," Andrea said. "I hope that's not an indication of how poor they are."

We ordered our usual scrambled eggs and toast after the waitress brought our coffee, decaf this time since we'd already had regular at the hotel. "I thought Claudia's question was interesting . . . you know, when she asked the sheriff if he thought Laszlo was murdered."

Andrea sipped her coffee thoughtfully before answering. "I don't think it's likely, even though a few people do seem to hold some things against him. Surely it isn't enough to result in murder."

"I keep wondering about Erika's relationship with Laszlo. She spent some days hiking with him in the Black Forest. This was before she met Franz. And did you notice when the minister said Stefan's name at the wedding that his middle name is Laszlo?"

"I noticed."

"Good grief! I just happened to think! Do you suppose Laszlo's Stefan's father?"

Andrea laughed. "I'm afraid that's a little far-fetched."

The waitress arrived with our food, and we turned our attention to the scrambled eggs. After we finished, I continued, "It's too bad Willard isn't here to update us on what they found in Laszlo's room."

"Maybe tomorrow. We can always count on Willard to fill us in on what's going on."

"I keep wondering just how rich Laszlo was, and who's going to get his money. I don't mean to sound mercenary, but wouldn't it be nice if some of it goes to Stefan?"

Andrea motioned to the waitress for more coffee. "I gather Laszlo's never been married. I suppose it would be logical if he left his money to Franz. We've never heard of any other siblings, so I assume it's just the two of them."

"Franz did seem quite distressed about Laszlo's death. Erika did, too."

The waitress came, refilled our cups, and left us with more half and half. We sat back to enjoy a final cup of decaf. "I've been so preoccupied with the death that I didn't even think about trying to notify Stefan and Maggie," I said.

"I thought about it, but they'd probably left the hotel in Charleston by the time we knew what had happened, and they were so secretive about their destination. I decided we should just let them enjoy their honeymoon, and they'll have to find out about it when they return. The sheriff asked me about their plans, and I told him all I knew, but of course that didn't help him much."

"Do you suppose he'll try to track them down?"

"I don't know. I hope not. They work so hard at the ski school and the hotel, they deserve a break."

I finished my coffee. "Of course, if it turns out Laszlo was murdered and Stefan is one of his heirs, the sheriff may want to get him back here for questioning right away. I hope that's not going to be the case."

#

We returned to the hotel because we couldn't decide how to spend the day. It was a wonderful sunny morning, but I think what we really wanted to do was hang out at the hotel and check on happenings there. Give Andrea any hint of a mystery, and she'll be on top of it till it's solved.

We went to our room for our books. "Do you suppose the sheriff and his deputies are still in Laszlo's room?" I asked.

"I don't know, but let's go to the lobby and read. I'll ask Ivy whether she's seen them come down. I'm also wondering if she's seen Juliet Gorsky."

Andrea went to the desk while I sat down on one of the chairs by the fireplace. The hotel was so quiet, I could hear her talking to Ivy. "Have you seen the sheriff and deputies come down from Laszlo's room?"

"No, they're still up there, I think. I did leave for a minute to use the bathroom in one of the rooms that was vacated, and I suppose they could have come down then."

"What about Juliet Gorsky, the woman who was with Laszlo last night?"

"I haven't seen her, either. All the young people checked out early this morning, but I don't suppose she's still in the attic. We're planning to put her in one of the vacant rooms if she's going to stay on."

"Have Asbury and David come back?"

"I haven't seen them, so I suppose they're still unloading chairs at the rental place. Look out through the kitchen and see if the truck's back there where they park it."

Andrea pulled the paper we'd found under the picnic table from her pocket. "It's just that we found this, and we thought it might belong to David. It's possible he and Nicole were exchanging email addresses, which is harmless enough."

Ivy gave a nervous little laugh. "As long as that's all they're exchanging."

Andrea went through the kitchen and looked out a window at the back. When she returned, "No truck yet."

Just then the sheriff and his men came down the stairs. Willard was carrying a cardboard box. He looked at us and nodded, and the look on his face said he was just dying to tell us some important news. We knew this would have to wait, because the sheriff would never approve of Willard spreading information about what was found at what might be a crime scene.

We sat and read a while. Andrea had an Alan Furst novel, and I was reading one of Ben Rehder's humorous mysteries, *Holy Moly*. "Why don't I go to the kitchen and put on a small pot of coffee?" I asked no one in particular, and without waiting for an answer, I did just that. "When Asbury comes back, maybe he can watch the desk for a while and you can join us," I said to Ivy. Of course, I was thinking there must be some leftover wedding cake that should be eaten. Maggie had cut a couple of pieces for the freezer so they could eat it on their anniversary, but the rest of it would get stale if we didn't finish it.

I used the small twelve-cup pot, and the coffee had just finished dripping through when Asbury walked in the back door. He took over at the desk when we promised to bring him coffee and cake, and Ivy fixed up a small tray for him complete with a napkin left over from the wedding.

The three of us sat down at a small table in the corner with our cake and coffee. Ivy started right in telling us about an experience last night. "I got up to go to the bathroom about two o'clock, and I noticed a light on in Mr. Novacek's room. I thought probably he couldn't sleep and was reading, or that maybe he just got up to go to the bathroom, too. I think now maybe he was having a problem, and maybe I could have done something."

"You had no way of knowing," Andrea said. "Could you tell what light was on?"

"I think it must have been the lamp between the beds. The overhead light would have been brighter."

"When it gets dark tonight, I'll go up to his room and turn on the light between the beds. We'll get on the phone to each other, and you tell me if it looks the same. What's your phone number?"

Ivy recited it, and Andrea took her cell phone from her pocket and put the number in her phone book.

"But Andrea, they still have that yellow tape across the door. I don't think you can go in there."

I knew yellow tape would never deter Andrea, but I didn't say so. Instead, I said, "Why don't you call the sheriff and ask him to go in with you. We don't know, but that light being on might be important."

"I'll do that." Andrea hit a few buttons on her phone and began explaining the situation to the sheriff.

While she was talking, Eva Weiss came into the kitchen. She looked like someone out of a fashion magazine that morning—hair and makeup perfect and wearing designer jeans and a light sweater. "I just heard the news about Laszlo. I can't believe it. I came over to pay my condolences to Stefan and Maggie, if they're back yet."

I'm sure you did, I thought, and on the spur of the moment I decided a white lie was in order since I didn't want to admit it hadn't occurred to me to contact the kids till it was too late. "They're not here. They wanted to keep their honeymoon plans secret, and they had left the Marriott by the time we tried to get in touch with them. They said they wouldn't have their cell phones on. They wanted time to themselves."

"I must go and speak to Franz and Erika. Excuse me."

Gladly, I thought as she left the kitchen and turned down the hallway. She must have already asked Asbury for their room number. I got up and brought the coffeepot over and gave everyone a refill to go with what was left of our cake. There was still a little in the pot, so I went to the desk and gave the rest to Asbury.

I just turned away from the desk when the front door opened and Juliet Gorsky walked in. She was dressed in a warm-up suit and sneakers, and she looked radiant. "I've just been hiking on one of the trails at Blackwater Falls," she said.

"I saw the most charming small waterfall. The trail crossed over it, and I was able to get pictures after the trail curved and I could look back on the falls and the bridge over it." She pulled a small camera from her pocket as if she intended to show me her photos.

I put my hand on her arm. "I'm very sorry to tell you this, but Laszlo passed away last night. He was found in bed this morning by the maid. His body has been taken by the medical examiner in order to determine cause of death."

Her face turned white, and she walked to the fireplace and sat down on one of the chairs. "I was hoping . . ." her voice dwindled to nothing, and she never said what she was hoping, much to my regret. I realized that she wasn't talking to me, but to herself.

#

Andrea invited the sheriff to eat supper with us, and we sat around the kitchen eating as much as we could hold of the leftover ham, potato salad, baked beans, and fruit salad. David had joined us, and Andrea showed him the paper we found. "I must have dropped that," he said, and reached out and took it from her without looking at her.

It was dark by the time we finished eating and cleaning up the kitchen. Asbury took the desk again, and Ivy went to the house and took their cordless phone to the window in their bedroom. Andrea and Ward went upstairs, and I followed them, stopping at the door to Laszlo's room while they went under the tape and inside.

Andrea had dialed Ivy, and Ward turned on the overhead light. "She says that isn't it," Andrea said.

He turned it off and switched on the lamp on the nightstand. "She says that's the one," Andrea said. "I don't know if it will ever have any significance, but at least we know."

Ward chuckled. "You wouldn't like a job with the Tucker County Sheriff's Department, would you?"

"I imagine that would be a snap, compared to teaching math to high school students."

"It'd be a tossup. We could use you if you ever decide you want to go back to work."

He sounded serious. When we were here in January, I had hoped that Andrea and the sheriff might become interested in each other, and then I began having second thoughts. What if they became seriously involved, got married, and Andrea left Pine Summit? What would I do without her? Now I was having the same mixed feelings. I hurried downstairs, because I had been meaning to talk to Ivy ever since morning and the discovery of Laszlo's body.

She was just coming through the back door into the kitchen, heading for the desk to relieve Asbury. I stopped her as she entered the lobby. "Ivy, I keep wondering what you make of the fact that Laszlo died on the night of the full moon? We were all hoping for such happiness and good fortune."

"These things happen, and there's no explaining them. But you know what they say: 'Everything happens for the best.'"

I'd heard that saying many times, but somehow I couldn't see how the death of a relative of the groom could be for the best, even if it meant Stefan inherited a lot of money. I nodded and didn't say anything more, not knowing what to say.

Andrea and Ward came downstairs, and she walked with him to his car. We said goodnight to Ivy and went to our room, where I immediately said to Andrea, "Did the sheriff tell you anything more about what happened to Laszlo, or what they found in his room?"

She hesitated for a moment. "This is strictly between us. He didn't say I shouldn't tell you. They found two copies of Laszlo's will in the room. He said they haven't had a chance to review them thoroughly, but I have a feeling he's gotten the gist of what they say."

"I wonder why Laszlo would have two copies of his will with him. Do you suppose he was planning to give a copy to Franz and Stefan? Maybe he had a premonition." Then I had another thought. "You don't suppose it was a suicide. He seemed cheerful, at least as long as we knew him."

"No telling. Ward didn't say anything else about the will, though. He did mention that they've been trying to reach Stefan and Maggie. They checked the Charleston airport to see if they flew out of there, and they didn't. He said he feels they should be informed of Laszlo's death right away. I disagreed with him about that, but he's the sheriff, after all."

When we finally went to bed, I found myself wishing for the feeling of peace and contentment I'd had the night before. I'd felt that with Maggie and Stefan married and enjoying themselves on a honeymoon, all was right with the world. Laszlo's death had left me with a feeling that everything definitely wasn't right.

CHAPTER FOUR

We woke up to a drizzly morning to match our mood. "I had been thinking it might be fun to go to the top on the ski lift today, but not if this continues," Andrea said. "I want to see the great view from up there again, and this time in the daylight."

"Forget that. You're never going to get me on that ski lift again." We were stuck on the lift when we were here in January, and finally rescued after nearly freezing to death.

Andrea just looked at me and shook her head. She's much more venturesome than I am, and always has been. After all, when she struck out for the university soon after high school graduation, with a small stash of baby-sitting money and no job, she managed to work her way through college in three years. I've always been a housewife and homebody; an occasional trip to the Canaan Valley is about all the adventure I can stand.

"Maybe it'll clear up. Let's go have breakfast, and when we're through we can see what kind of a day it's going to be."

"Let's go to the lodge. Willard seems to go there every morning, and maybe he'll be there today. I'm dying to know what was in Laszlo's will, and I have no doubt he'll tell us."

We got dressed and went to the lobby, where we said hello and goodbye to Ivy. By the time we got to the lodge, it was raining harder, and we got an umbrella from the backseat of Andrea's car and huddled under it on our way to the entrance. No sheriff's car could be seen in the parking lot, but we could hope Willard would arrive later.

We both decided on French toast—it was just that kind of morning. We drank coffee while we waited for our food and for Willard to show up. We had more coffee when we finished eating and were just about ready to get up and pay when he walked in. Of course, he came right over and sat down beside us. "I hope you don't mind if I join you."

"Of course not," I said, and when the waitress came to take his order, we asked for a third cup of coffee. No way were we going to leave when we had the chief gossip of Tucker County seated at our table.

Willard ordered his usual coffee and biscuits, and when the waitress left, Andrea said, "Have you found Maggie and Stefan yet?"

"Not yet. They didn't fly out of the Charleston airport; that much we know. Of course, as usual, you know anything I tell you is strictly confidential."

"Of course," we both assured him.

"We have to assume they're still driving the Volvo, and law officers are looking for them all over the area. It's just that the sheriff feels they should be notified of the uncle's death."

The waitress brought Willard's order and poured more coffee for us. I couldn't help wondering if there was more to it than that, and what Willard said next made me even surer that there was.

He had devoured one biscuit, and he took a deep breath. I'm not sure what is more important to Willard—eating or impressing two elderly ladies with what he knows. "Laszlo's will has proven to be most interesting. Like I said, this is strictly confidential, but your niece is married to Stefan and I know you'd want to know. The deceased was a very wealthy man, and a large part of his estate will go to Stefan. Some goes to his brother, too, but the bulk goes to Stefan."

I looked at Andrea, wondering if she was thinking what I was thinking. Maybe my idea that Laszlo was Stefan's father wasn't so far-fetched after all. Of course, her face was the usual well-composed mask, revealing nothing. She'd make a great poker player, I always tell her. I couldn't help feeling a little thrill at the thought of Stefan inheriting so much money.

"Has the medical examiner arrived at a cause of death?" Andrea asked.

Willard leaned toward us. "It definitely was his heart. It didn't appear to be diseased, but something happened there. There'll be more testing. In the meantime, we're trying to find out what medications he took. We didn't find anything in his room. His brother and sister-in-law don't know of any, and he doesn't have other family members—except for Stefan, that is.

"We found some herbal tea in his room, and a little electric pot for heating water, but the interesting thing is, there was no cup in the room. Of course we took the tea for testing." Willard had finished his second biscuit and coffee by this time, and was signaling for a refill.

"I suppose Ward mentioned to you that Ivy saw a light in his room at around two o'clock. It was the bedside lamp."

"Yes, he told me all about it. There was something else the medical examiner discovered . . ." Willard took time to clear his throat. His face was turning red. He leaned even closer. "There was evidence of sexual activity."

"Then someone was with him in the room," I said, hoping Willard wouldn't fill us in on any details about how they knew there was sexual activity.

"Probably, but not necessarily."

Now my face was turning red. Andrea was simply looking thoughtful, analyzing all these facts.

We left the restaurant and went back to the hotel in the rain. Asbury had started a fire in the fireplace, and we decided it would be a good day to stay in and read. "It's a good time to keep an eye on the lobby," Andrea said.

We took our jackets and purses to our room. "If it turns out Laszlo was murdered, who do you think did it?" I asked.

"It's too early to speculate. There were various people who had a reason to dislike him. Claudia and Agnes showed the most animosity toward him. The Beckers lost their life savings because of him. They avoided him, but they didn't seem so openly antagonistic. Franz and Erika seemed very upset by his death, but I did find it puzzling that she so matter-of-factly referred to her relationship with Laszlo before she knew Franz when we were at Cathedral State Park. Then there's Juliet. I'm not sure anyone knows anything about her."

"Her face turned white when I told her about Laszlo's death, and she seemed truly disturbed. If it was an act, she's an amazing actor." I picked up my book. "Of course, we both know Maggie and Stefan had nothing to do with it."

"Of course. Let's just hope the sheriff knows it, too. The fact that Laszlo was still alive and having a fine time at the reception when they left should count for something."

Andrea opened the door, ready to go to the lobby, and we could hear Franz and Erika talking in their room across from us. It was evident they were arguing. What wasn't evident was exactly what they were saying. Their voices were louder than usual, but muffled. Her voice was clearer than his, and it sounded as if she moved closer to the door. Then we heard her say, "I'm going shopping, and I don't care what you think."

He said something about "credit cards," then started speaking in what I figured was Czech.

Of course, we were standing there listening, spellbound.

"We agreed to speak nothing but English while we were here!" she shouted.

His voice was getting louder now, too. "The hell with English!" Then he was ranting in Czech again.

Their doorknob rattled, and Andrea pushed me back into our room and closed our door softly.

We could hear their door open, and Erika, standing right outside our door, said, "You're not going to be able to deny me the things I want any longer!" She slammed the door, and we could hear her going down the hall.

Nothing much surprises Andrea, but her mouth fell open just as mine did. "Sounds like she knows they're going to have money now, and she intends to spend it," I whispered.

"You'd assume from the conversation that they know about the will. Laszlo may have discussed it with them years ago, for all we know. You'd also assume that maybe he's a tightwad, and maybe she's felt deprived for years. Or it may be the other way around, and she's a big spender who's given him a lot of financial problems."

We waited a few minutes, then went to the lobby, closing the door softly behind us and hoping Franz wouldn't know we were anywhere around, listening to their argument. Ivy motioned to us to come to the desk. "What the heck's the matter with Frau Novacek? She went stomping out of here like she was furious."

"They seemed to be having an argument," Andrea said. "We could hear loud voices coming from their room. I suppose it's a stressful time for them, what with Laszlo's death, and Stefan and Maggie being out of touch."

"I'm sure it is. But where's she going in this rain? Seems like a good day to stay in by the fire."

"That's what we plan to do. Are there enough leftovers for supper tonight?" I asked.

"For you two, yes. The rest of them are on their own. Maybe it'll clear up by evening and they can all go out without any problems."

We heard someone coming through the kitchen, and David came into the lobby and to the desk. "I'm going back to play video games with the girls."

"Just leave the door to the room open while you're back there."

"Mom! I'm not a baby who has to be watched all the time."

"Maybe it's the girls who have to be watched with a good-looking kid like you," Andrea said, obviously trying to lighten up the situation.

He turned to Andrea. "I don't appreciate you spying on me, either."

"I wasn't spying. The moon was almost full, and we wanted to see the side lawn in the moonlight. Have you ever noticed how beautiful it is around here when there's a clear sky and a full moon? Anyway, I saw you and Nicole out there, and like I told you in January, parents need to know where their teenagers are at all times. And what they're doing. That's the reason I told your mother we saw you and the reason for the open door."

Math teachers, even retired ones, have this air of authority that squelches arguments from the most rebellious teenagers. David smiled just a little, and I got the impression that he was embarrassed to admit to the girls that he had to leave the door open, but on the other hand he was glad so many people cared about him and what he was doing.

"By the way," I said, "don't you need a television to play video games?"

"They have a PSP. I'll leave the door open."

He went on down the hall, leaving me wondering what a PSP is.

Andrea put another log on the fire, and we settled down with our books. We'd promised Ivy we'd put on a pot of coffee later, and she could join us in front of the fireplace, where she could keep an eye on the desk. She said they had no reservations, and might not have anyone else checking in till the weekend.

After reading for a couple of hours, I put on a small pot of coffee. We decided we'd better eat more cake. *It seemed it would never be eaten up, and that would be a shame*, I thought. I put three generous pieces on small plates with forks, and then loaded a tray with three cups of coffee and some creamer. None of us used sugar.

We'd hardly gotten settled down when the phone rang, and Ivy jumped up to answer it. "It's for Mr. Novacek. Would you get him, please?"

Andrea got up and went down the hall, and I could hear her knocking on Franz's door. She soon returned, and he followed. He went to the desk and began speaking Czech, or possibly it was German. I couldn't hear him that well, and might not have been able to tell the difference if I could.

Ivy came back and sat with us, and his conversation continued for a few minutes. He said "thank you" to Andrea as he passed us on his way back to his room. I was wondering if he and Erika had just made up over the phone. "Was that a woman?" I asked Ivy.

"No, it was a man. He had a heavy accent."

"Maybe someone from an embassy. He's a diplomat of some sort." Then I found myself wondering again whether Franz might be a spy. I've read a few of Andrea's international thrillers, and it seems that embassies are full of spies. What effect this would have on anything, I didn't know. It was just an interesting sidelight at this time.

"I can't help wondering why someone would be calling him on the hotel phone and not on his cell phone," Andrea said. Leave it to Andrea to ponder over every little thing.

"Were you able to find a room for Juliet Gorsky?" I asked Ivy.

"Yes, I put her in Room 5 down the West hallway, on the same side as Mr. and Mrs. Becker. David brought her suitcase down for her."

We had just gotten back to the coffee and cake when the front door opened. For a rainy day, there was a lot of activity going on. It was Erika, wearing a raincoat and loaded down with packages. She looked like she'd been having the time of her life. "Could I please have some of that coffee?"

"Certainly," Ivy said.

I got up right away. "I'll get it, Ivy. You need to listen for the phone. Would you like some of the leftover wedding cake?"

"That would be lovely. This will be a real rainy-day treat."

The shopping spree certainly had improved her mood, but that's what shopping sprees do. I took the tray to the kitchen and brought back coffee and cake for Erika. "Where's Asbury? We haven't seen him all day."

"He's at the house, trying to fix a drippy faucet. He's not much of a plumber, and he usually works on these things with Stefan, but the dripping started after Stefan left."

I turned to Erika. "You've been shopping, obviously. Did you go to Davis?"

"I went on down to Elkins. They have some lovely shops there. I don't know how I'll get all this home, and maybe I'll have to ship some of it. Of course, we don't know what our plans are at the moment. We'll have to plan some sort of memorial service for Laszlo, probably back in Prague, where he had his headquarters. We hope to have his body cremated and take his ashes with us."

"That sounds like a practical plan," Andrea said.

I didn't know what else to add, so I said, "Would anyone like more cake?" I was hoping I wouldn't be the only one who wanted more.

"I'd love another piece," Erika said.

She and Willard would become good friends if she stayed around here, I thought. As a matter of fact, since we were serving food, I expected him to pop through the door at any minute. I got up and put four more pieces on the plate.

"There's still so much left, maybe we should consider donating some to a local nursing home or something," Andrea said, and I found myself hoping there was no nearby nursing home for donating cake.

"I'll call the kids. I'm sure they'll take care of some of it." Ivy got up and went down the hall.

I was sitting where I could see all the way to the end of the west wing, and I was surprised and pleased to see that one of the doors down that way was open, and David had done just as he said he would. Then the door across from that one opened, and Klaus and Karla came out just as the others did. They all followed Ivy down the hallway, and before long the kids were sitting on the stairs with cake and milk. Klaus brought two folding chairs from the small table in the kitchen, and he and Karla had cake and coffee, too.

Franz didn't come out to join us, and the sisters didn't show up, nor did Juliet. Everyone finally went to their rooms. Ivy, Andrea and I carried the dishes to the kitchen and started washing them. "When you're ready for supper, come to the kitchen and fill a plate." Ivy said. "You can take it to your room if you want, or just eat here in the kitchen, since we're not inviting the others."

We went to our room for a short nap, which turned out to be quite a bit longer than we intended. It was eight o'clock when we finally went back to the lobby. Ivy wasn't behind the desk, but we heard a door close upstairs. "She must be using one of the bathrooms up there," Andrea said. "Everyone checked out of upstairs yesterday. Or possibly Hadley's cleaning, but I wouldn't think she'd be here this late."

At that moment, Ivy appeared from the hallway to our left. "Too much coffee. I had to use the bathroom down there."

"Is Hadley still here?" I asked

"No, she left hours ago? Why? Did you need something?"

"No, but we heard a noise upstairs."

"There's no one up there. Everyone from that floor checked out."

Andrea didn't waste any time—she went to the stairs and started climbing, so I followed her. She got to the top and looked down both hallways, then reached across the tape and opened Laszlo's door. She stooped under the tape and went in, and I did likewise. "Somebody's been in here," she said. "The room wasn't this much of a mess when we came last evening to see which light had been on the night before. I suppose it's possible the deputies came back and stirred things up some more, but I don't think so."

"We definitely heard someone up here, and they didn't come down the stairs, so where are they?"

She went back into the hall. "I don't know, but I'm going to find out. You stay in the hallway and watch while I check out the rooms and bathrooms."

The hall remained quiet as she checked the rooms in the one wing, and then started down the other. Maggie's and Stefan's rooms were locked, but everything else was unlocked. The situation was getting eerier by the minute for me, and I wished she'd hurry. Andrea said, "There's only one other way out of here, and that's the attic staircase. Go downstairs to the kitchen and keep an eye on the laundry room door. I'll check out the attic and everything else on the way down."

I was eager to go downstairs because the dim and deserted hallway felt a little creepy, but I wasn't happy about her going up to the attic alone. "It's possible that when they heard us coming up the stairs, they ran out that way before we reached the top. They could have gone out the back door from the kitchen."

"Go on down. I'll come down the attic stairs."

Ivy was looking puzzled when I came downstairs. "What's going on?"

"Nothing, as far as we can tell. We didn't find anyone up there. I have to go to the kitchen—Andrea's coming down the attic stairs."

It occurred to me that those stairs would be dark, and we certainly hadn't bothered to take flashlights with us. I knew what I had to do was go in and turn on the laundry room light and open the door to the stairs, so at least a little light would help Andrea find her way down. But what if someone was lurking in the laundry room, or worse yet, behind the stairs? Better that I encounter them with some light available than Andrea in the dark, so I went to the door of the laundry, opened it, and switched on the light. Nothing. I tiptoed over to the door to the attic stairs and opened it.

I could hear someone coming down the stairs, and I resisted the impulse to run for my life. "Andrea?"

"Yes. Thanks for the light. I was feeling my way down the stairs."

"Did you find anything?"

"Nothing. And you saw nothing, I suppose."

"No, all was quiet. It's time to quit playing detective. Let's just wash up at the kitchen sink. Then we can help ourselves to some food."

"I'll ask Ivy if she wants a plate."

I was washing my hands when Andrea came back, and she came to the sink when I was through. "Ivy ate earlier with Asbury and David. The rain stopped and everyone else went out, so she said we should feel free to eat in here or in the lobby if we want."

"The lobby's always nice when there's a fire going."

We put the last of the ham, potato salad, and fruit salad on our plates. The baked beans and crudités were already gone. "I'm going back to Laszlo's room and look around," Andrea said between bites. "Someone was in there, I'm sure of it. They were looking for something, or possibly trying to steal something. Maybe we scared them away, and whatever they were looking for is still in there."

"Why don't you go ahead?" I said when we'd finished. "I'll clean up the kitchen and join you." I washed up all the containers that held the food as well as our dishes, and by the time I was through it was nine o'clock. I went through the lobby and told Ivy where I was going, and then headed up the stairs.

Andrea had left the door open and the overhead light on in the room, and she was pulling out drawers and looking through their contents. "I called Ward, and he said no one was back in the room since we were there checking out the lights last night. He's coming to join us in a little while."

I helped her check the drawers, and we found nothing but clothes in the chest. I felt around on the shelf in the closet, and Andrea looked in the drawer of the nightstand. It's no wonder the sheriff would like to offer her a job—she's probably more thorough than any deputy on his staff. She reached to the farthest corner of the drawer and pulled out something that looked like a checkbook. "I'd better not open it till Ward gets here. He might want to check it for fingerprints." She laid it carefully on top of the nightstand.

We heard voices from downstairs, and shortly the sheriff joined us. "This was in the back of the nightstand drawer," Andrea said. "It must be a checkbook"

Ward picked it up immediately, holding it by the edges, and began going through it. "Interesting . . ."

I was straining my neck to see what he was finding so interesting, without any luck. Andrea, not being one to waste any time, said, "What are you finding?"

He held the book so we both could see it. "A month ago, he wrote a check for two thousand something or other, maybe marks, or possibly korunas, to Klaus Becker."

"If it's korunas, it wouldn't be worth much," Andrea said.

How they knew so much about European currency, I had no idea. Neither was a world traveler. I elected not to say something that would reveal my ignorance.

"I wonder why he'd be writing a check to Becker," Ward said.

"You realize of course that Klaus Becker and Erika Novacek are brother and sister," Andrea said.

"Yes, but that doesn't explain the check."

"I know it doesn't, but something else that might be of interest to you is this: From what we hear, Klaus invested a great deal in one of Laszlo's ventures and lost everything. Even his children's college funds were involved."

Ward nodded. "Interesting."

"And while we're telling you what we know about the family's history, we might as well tell you about Claudia and Agnes. Again, this is third-hand information, but we hear that Agnes was engaged to Laszlo many years ago. Claudia had an affair with him, and the engagement was called off. Apparently Claudia and Agnes eventually patched things up, but now they both hate Laszlo. Or I should say, hated him."

"You're just a regular fountain of information tonight."

"Agnes was Stefan's nanny when he was young. I don't know whether that has any significance, but thought you might like to know."

"I had heard that. About her being the nanny, that is. I'll take this checkbook along with me. Thanks for finding it."

"Anything new from the medical examiner?" Andrea asked.

"Not yet. We should know something in a few days. How long are you planning to stay?"

"We're not sure. We're in no hurry to get home."

I knew without asking that we'd be in the valley till the cause of death was determined, and if it was a murder, till it was solved. Andrea can't resist digging into a mystery, and I must say, I was finding the situation fascinating myself. Besides, it would be nice to be there when the kids got home. Like everyone else, I was wondering where they were and why they'd been so difficult to find. They didn't fly out of Charleston, so they had driven somewhere.

They're both such athletic types—ski instructors, Ski Patrol, and hiking in the summer—that I'd been doing some detective thinking of my own. My guess was that they were hiking on the Appalachian Trail somewhere. It wouldn't be the ideal honeymoon for most people, but for Maggie and Stefan, it would be perfect. It seems that an old, pale blue Volvo would be the easiest thing in the world to spot, but like Andrea, I was cheering them on, hoping they'd get to complete two weeks of honeymooning before they were intercepted. The fascinating thing was, Stefan was rich and they didn't know it yet. And I couldn't help hoping the sheriff had the same idea, that Stefan was rich and was completely unaware of the fact that Lazlo was dead and he was the primary heir.

CHAPTER FIVE

Ivy finally had enough free time on Wednesday to go to lunch with us, and we took her to the Blackwater Lodge, since we had taken her to the Canaan Lodge on our previous trip. Of course, we did the ritual walk down to see the falls, which Ivy found most enthralling. She hadn't been there since she was a child. Andrea whipped out her camera and took bunches of photos, and I managed to snap one of the two of them, then Andrea took one of the three of us in front of the falls. She showed us a tiny card inside the camera, and said she'd take that card to WalMart and have some pictures printed. It's truly a brave new world, and I'm a scaredy-cat, not brave at all when it comes to electronics.

I struggled back up the stairs; even Ivy, who mostly sits behind a desk these days, was less out-of-breath than I was. She's younger, I rationalized, and it hasn't been that long since she was getting plenty of exercise cleaning the hotel. I collapsed into the backseat of the car, wanting room to spread out and catch my breath.

The restaurant was crowded, but we did get a table by a window, the last one available. We'd walk out onto the patio later so Ivy could get a better view of the Blackwater Canyon. We were just considering our menus when we saw Erika, Claudia, and Agnes follow the hostess to a table. We couldn't ask them to join us, because we were sitting at a table for four, but we smiled and waved. The hostess seated them at a table that was, unfortunately, too far away for us to hear their conversation.

We all decided on a salad, and were sipping our iced tea when we heard raised voices from the direction of our hotel-mates' table. I couldn't help looking their way, and Claudia and Agnes were both staring at Erika. The argument continued, and I heard the word "Laszlo." It was the sisters whose voices were raised, I realized, or maybe it was just Claudia, making enough noise for the three of them.

"What in the world can they be arguing about," Ivy said. "I'd think such refined ladies would know better than to act like that."

I couldn't help thinking that Ivy, as uneducated as she was, would know how to behave better than the three at the other table did. "I can't imagine. I heard the word Laszlo."

Andrea didn't say anything but just sat there taking it all in. Claudia and Agnes got up, snatched up their purses, and stalked out, staring straight ahead. Finally Andrea said, "I think I must go over and ask Erika to sit with us. If she's not too upset to stay, that is."

Andrea went to Erika's table and appeared to speak for a moment, and Erika nodded her head. She said a few words to the waitress and followed Andrea to our table.

She leaned down and hugged me, and then also gave Ivy an awkward hug, as if one person hugged at a table meant everyone must be hugged.

"So nice to see you," she said, "and to be able to join you." She was smiling as if she'd just been through the most tranquil experience of her life.

She's a true diplomat's wife, it seemed to me. I wondered if Franz knows how lucky he is. Much as I wanted to know what transpired at the other table, I didn't dare ask. Andrea would have given me that stare of hers that says no matter how curious we are, and she's a curious person too, we don't stray beyond the bounds of propriety.

Erika looked stunning in a red dress that flattered her fair skin, blue eyes, and blond curls. So instead of questioning her about the fracas at their table, I said, "You look wonderful today. Red is your color."

"Thanks. I found this dress when I was shopping Monday. I do love red."

Andrea changed the subject. "How is Franz doing? We haven't seen him since the day of Laszlo's death."

"He's taking it very hard. It was just the two of them, and they've always been close. He's turned his cell phone off and doesn't want to talk to anyone. I haven't been able to drag him out of our room, but I told him he's taking me to dinner tonight. I'm tired of bringing food in to him. I'd ask you to go along, but I think maybe he'll do better with just the two of us."

That explained why Franz received a call on the hotel phone, and I was sure Andrea was thinking the same thing. The waitress brought salads all around, and this time Erika's was much smaller than everyone else's. "Just having a garden salad, since we're eating out tonight."

I was beginning to understand how Erika kept her wonderfully trim figure. A tiny meal one time and a big one the next could explain it. I don't care how many times I'm eating out; I'm having more than a tiny garden salad for lunch. I tried to think of a subject to talk about that might bring up interesting information without appearing to pry. Then I hit on a possible way to learn more about Amalie and Nicole. "David is enjoying having the girls in the hotel. They were playing video games the other day. He has some school friends in the valley, but I think they're too far away for them to enjoy seeing a lot of each other in the summer. They're all too young to drive."

"Oh, the girls are crazy about David. He's so cute. Nicole is wishing him to be a few years older, so she could consider him a boyfriend."

Ivy looked as if she enjoyed the remark about how cute David is, but was thankful he wasn't a few years older.

Nicole was more cheerful now that she had gotten acquainted with David, so I didn't feel she was such a threat to him as I had originally, when she looked like the typical rebellious teenager. "I think they're exchanging email addresses so they can stay in touch. It seems to be a wonderful thing, the way messages can be sent all over the world without having to pay a phone bill."

Erika stopped nibbling on her salad for a moment. "Do you have email?"

"No, but Andrea does. Trying to figure out a computer would be too much for me."

"I'll give you my email address," Andrea said.

"And I'll give you mine. It'll be fun to stay in touch. We can share pictures. Are you on Facebook?"

"No, are you?"

"Yes. You should join. It's a good way to stay in touch."

"I'll think about it. I'll let you know if I decide to do it."

On that friendly note we finished our food and called for a refill of iced tea. Erika added a bit of sugar substitute to hers. "Has anyone told you Laszlo's partner is to arrive today?"

Andrea looked puzzled. "No, I didn't know Laszlo had a partner."

"He's not really an official partner, I guess. It's just that they participated in some business ventures together. They've been friends for a long time. We won't be having a service here, but he felt the need to be here."

"I took a reservation for a John Fuller this morning, and that's the only one we've had," Ivy said. "I didn't know he was connected to Mr. Novacek."

"Yes, that's the one. He's from London. We see him there occasionally. We called him when we found out about Laszlo, being sure he'd want to know."

I'd been dying to ask Erika what she knew about Juliet Gorsky, and I could resist no longer. "Did you know Miss Gorsky before she arrived at the hotel?"

"No, we'd never heard of her. All we can figure is that she was a new girlfriend of Laszlo's. We're not sure why she showed up at the Alpenhof."

Andrea nodded, and for once, she looked as if she were glad I'd been nosy. We finished our tea and went out onto the patio for a view of the canyon. Erika looked nostalgic as she leaned on the railing and gazed into the depths below. "This reminds me of a wonderful Rhine River cruise I enjoyed many years ago. Of course, the Blackwater River doesn't have castles and vineyards, but there's just something about this valley that made me think of the other one."

Was she with Laszlo, Franz, or someone else on that cruise? The only way I could think of to find out was to ask, "How long since you cruised the Rhine?"

"It's been at least thirty years. I rarely get back to Germany these days, since we're stationed at one diplomatic post or another all the time."

Since Stefan is twenty-seven, that was well before he was born. The information she gave didn't answer my question, but I couldn't think of a tactful way to find out more. We left the patio and went back through the lodge.

As we were getting into our cars, Erika said, "I'm going shopping. The sisters were supposed to go with me, but as you saw, that didn't work out." She gave a quick laugh and drove away.

We went back to the hotel, where Ivy relieved Asbury at the desk. "Let's get our books and sit in the lobby and read," I said. "Then we can get a look at John Fuller when he arrives."

Ivy motioned for us to come to the desk. "Mr. Fuller checked in earlier. Asbury put him down on the wing with the Beckers, across from Ms. Gorsky, since your side is full. I hope those teenagers aren't too noisy for him."

"Oh, well," I said, "let's get our books and read in the lobby anyway. Who knows what excitement will occur. We'll have cake and coffee later."

"I'll get the books," Andrea said. "I don't think we're ever going to finish that cake. We can save some for Maggie and Stefan when they get back."

"I wonder if they've been located yet. I think the sheriff would let us know if they'd been found."

She started down the hall. "I'm sure he will."

#

We'd been reading for a couple of hours. "I'll make coffee," I called to Ivy. "We'll have some more of the cake."

"Wonderful! I could use a break, and nothing's happening here."

By the time the coffee dripped, a tall thin man in slacks and a tweed blazer walked into the lobby from the Becker wing. This had to be John Fuller. He appeared to be somewhat younger than Laszlo—mid-fifties, I guessed. "Good afternoon," Andrea said. "I'm Andrea Flynn, Maggie's aunt, and this is my sister, Kathleen Williamson. Ivy McGee is the lady behind the desk."

"I'm delighted to meet you. I'm John Fuller." He shook hands with all of us.

"Would you like to have some coffee and cake with us? We're finishing up the wedding cake."

"That would be very nice. Could I help with something?"

The man had a fascinating accent. I think it's what's known as scouse, but then what do I know about English accents? "Just have a seat. Won't take but a minute." I went to the kitchen and got everything ready, then returned with a tray. Ivy joined us.

John took a cup of coffee and began stirring creamer into it. "I've been looking at my guidebook for the area. There are several interesting attractions I'd like to see. I'm going to persuade Franz to go with me. Erika said he's feeling down about Laszlo's death, and hasn't been out at all. I think it would do him good to go over to Blackwater Falls. We could see the falls, then have tea in the restaurant."

"An excellent idea," Andrea said. "I think that might revive his spirits."

"Lord knows we all need that now and then," John said.

We finished our coffee, and he helped me carry the things to the kitchen before he went down the hall and knocked on Franz's door. Soon the two of them came back through, chatting intently, and seeming not to see us. Just at the door, John turned and gave a thumbs-up sign.

It was after four when Willard walked in, still in uniform. He came and sat with us at the fireplace, all smiles. "I just called Hadley. She's coming down when she's through cleaning, and we're going out to eat."

I couldn't help thinking Willard was going in his uniform, knowing that Hadley was one of those women who are impressed by uniforms. "You're off duty for the day?"

"Yep. Got off at four. We're driving over to Elkins. Gonna eat at the Cheat River Inn. It's a very romantic place, has outdoor dining on a deck overlooking the river."

"That sounds wonderful. Maybe we should have supper there some evening, Andrea."

Willard leaned toward us. "I have news. We've located Maggie's car. It's in a shop in White Sulphur Springs. They had a water pump go out. The owner took them out to the airport to rent a car. He has no idea where they went from there."

"I suppose you have a description and license on the rental car," Andrea said.

I could tell from the look on her face she wasn't happy about the car being found, and I wasn't either. "We were hoping the kids would be able to go ahead and enjoy their honeymoon, and then deal with Laszlo's death when they got back."

"I know, but it's standard procedure in our office to track people down in a case like this." He leaned even closer after looking around to see who was listening. "There's news from the medical examiner, too. The deceased had ingested a lethal dose of digitalis. Foxglove. This is strictly confidential, of course. I'm thinking he got it in a cup of tea."

My heart was pounding with this news. "What about the tea bags that were in the room? Maybe someone back in Prague put something extra in his tea bags. Or substituted what was in them with the foxglove."

"That's possible, but we didn't find a cup in the room. Hadley said she didn't remove anything. She just went in there, saw him, and screamed. Someone must have been with him to remove the cup. Anyway, the tea bags are still being analyzed," Willard whispered, because Ivy was approaching.

"Hadley called the desk on her cell phone. She said she tried you, but you must have your phone off. She'll be ready in a minute. She's changing clothes."

Ivy went back to the desk, and I just had to get another question in before Hadley appeared. "The sheriff doesn't think Maggie or Stefan had anything to do with this, does he?" I was ready to do battle with anyone who might suspect them.

"Oh, no, no, I'm sure he doesn't think anything like that," Willard stammered. "He just wants them back here so they can be informed of Laszlo's death."

The gentleman doth protest too much, I thought.

CHAPTER SIX

We went to our room to get ready to go out somewhere to eat supper. "As usual, I'm amazed Willard gives us so much information. I'm sure some of that's supposed to be confidential. What do you think Ward would say if he knew?" I asked.

"I don't even want to think about it! Willard has a need to impress people. But I'm glad he divulges so much—at least we know what's going on."

"It sounds like Laszlo was murdered."

She nodded. "Unless it was suicide. That doesn't make sense, though, because of the missing teacup. Also, he didn't seem the least depressed. He certainly was having a great time grinning at the sisters, tormenting them."

"Of course the fact that he brought two copies of his will with him makes me wonder if his death might be a suicide."

"Not necessarily," Andrea said. "Maybe he simply wanted Franz and Stefan to have a copy. Maybe he was feeling his age and thought it was time for them to know his wishes."

I put on fresh lipstick and combed my hair. "I'm wondering about the sisters taking separate rooms. Maybe one of them insisted on it so she could slip out at night to murder him without the other knowing it."

Andrea laughed. "All we have to do is find out which one insisted on separate rooms, and we have our killer."

"They both have a motive, but I suppose it could have been an accident, especially if he was taking digitalis. Maybe he took one pill, then forgot and took another."

"They didn't find any medication in his room."

"Oh, that's right. It sounds like there's no other choice. Laszlo was murdered."

Andrea had finished changing. "We can't solve it tonight, so let's go eat. The lodge okay?"

"It's the handiest, and the food is wonderful. Let's go."

David was in the lobby dusting the furniture when we went through Friday morning. "Want to go have breakfast with us?" Andrea asked.

I was glad she did. We hadn't seen enough of David on this trip; he'd been too preoccupied with the teenage girls.

"I ate a bowl of cereal, and I have to finish this dusting."

"Is Hadley sick? She's not here to clean?"

David finished the coffee table and started on the mantle. "She had to take her little boy to the dentist this morning, so Mom thought we should help her out by dusting the lobby."

Ivy spoke up from behind the desk. "Go on, and I'll finish the dusting. Everything's quiet this morning. You know you want to have pancakes, if they're going to the lodge."

He grinned. "There's always room for pancakes."

He hopped into the backseat when we got to the car, and we took off.

"How's school going?" Andrea asked.

"Fine. I had a B average last year. Mom and Asbury insist on a B average or better."

"What's your favorite subject?"

"Math and the science classes. I hate English and history."

They chatted on about school till we were seated at the lodge restaurant. After ordering coffee and a Dr Pepper, Andrea took the subject further. "Where are you thinking about going to college?"

"The question should be, 'Am I thinking about going to college,' not where."

"Keep your grades up, and you should be able to get in, if that's what you're concerned about."

"It's more the money. Mom and Asbury aren't exactly rolling in it, you know."

Andrea thought a moment before speaking. "You're going into high school this fall, aren't you?"

"Yes, finally!"

"Work on keeping the grades up, and you might get a scholarship. Then, too, I have a feeling that there are plenty of people around who would be willing to help you if you're sincerely interested."

"Are you talking about Stefan and Maggie, and all the money they're going to get?"

Boy, news sure travels fast, I thought.

Andrea chuckled. "I'm not talking about anyone specific, but let's just say help is usually available to those who truly want it and deserve it."

"I wish I had it made like Amalie. She'll be able to go into her father's business when she finishes college."

We had learned in January that David's father was serving a long prison term for manslaughter, so he'd be no help. Ivy divorced him—"She wasn't about to stay married to a jailbird," as Asbury had told us.

"There are plenty of opportunities out there for someone who's intelligent and ambitious," Andrea said. "Since you're both, you don't have to rely on a ready-made career. You can be successful on your own."

The waitress came with our coffee, and we ordered breakfast. Andrea took a sip, then set her cup down. "What sort of business does Amalie's father have?"

"He has a drugstore. It wouldn't be the most interesting work for me, filling bottles with pills all day, but Amalie doesn't seem to mind the idea of doing it. She's kind of quiet, probably doesn't like too much excitement anyway. She already works there in the summer."

"So Amalie's studying to be a pharmacist?" I asked, thinking about Klaus Becker owning a drugstore and having access to all the digitalis he wanted. I was sure Andrea was thinking the same thing.

"Yes, she's going to be a pharmacist and join her dad. Nicole wouldn't want to do that. She wants to be an archeologist and go on digs. Sounds a lot more exciting, doesn't it?"

When we first met David, he would have said "don't it?" Andrea's prompting about his grammar must have done some good. "I think archeology would be really exciting," I said.

"If you went to WVU, you could come home on weekends for skiing," Andrea said.

"Yeah, I know. There's a ski area that's closer to Morgantown, too, but I've never checked it out. Jeremy and I are hoping to go there this winter if we can get someone to take us."

Jeremy is David's friend we met last trip. They spent every spare minute skiing, and David became a much better student because Ivy and Asbury would only allow him to ski if he kept his grades up.

Little by little, we were gathering information that would be helpful in figuring out who killed Laszlo. Andrea would tell the sheriff about the pharmacy—what he'd be able to do with that information, only time would tell.

#

Back in our room, I said, "Amazing what you can learn from a kid. Interesting, isn't it, that Klaus Becker is a druggist with access to all the digitalis he wants."

"Yes, and then there's that checkbook of Laszlo's, with a check made out to Klaus. How does that fit in?"

"Do you suppose Klaus was blackmailing Laszlo about something?"

Andrea chuckled. "I don't think blackmailers accept checks. They don't want evidence of their crime lying around."

"I had forgotten about the check made to Klaus, because it didn't seem all that important. No telling if it has any bearing on the murder."

"There's something else. Digitalis is derived from foxglove, and that would be easy for anyone to grow. Add some to herbal tea, and it could be fatal, especially if sex were involved, which causes an increase in heart rate even without help from a drug."

Andrea takes such a clinical attitude toward everything that nothing she says surprises me. "It certainly seems like the murderer was a woman, considering the circumstances," I said.

"Anything is possible till we know more."

Andrea was putting on her hiking boots, always a bad sign. She was going to try to talk me into doing something strenuous. "I'm determined to hike to the top of Seneca Rocks. Every time we come here, I put it off, but this time I'm going to do it."

I was incredulous. "You can't climb those rocks. What are you thinking?"

"You don't have to climb the rocks to reach the top. There's a trail. It's just a little over a mile long. You'd better come with me. We have all day, and we can take it easy."

"Thanks, but I'd rather take it easy right here with my book."

"Take your book with you, and you can read on a bench while I hike the trail. You'll get some fresh air and sunshine. Be good for you."

"Sunshine causes skin cancer."

"I have some sunscreen you can use."

I had run out of excuses, and actually, the idea of sitting on a bench in a beautiful area was appealing. "Okay, but don't expect me to walk far. Maybe we can find a place in Harman to have coffee when we're through."

Andrea laughed. "Maybe we should just come back here and have coffee and try to eat up some more of that cake."

I had to agree. It certainly would be a shame to waste wedding cake. Besides, who knew what interesting interaction among guests might be going on in the lobby?

#

Europeans are much more athletic than the average American, I thought, as we arrived at Seneca Rocks and Andrea took out her binoculars and scanned the trail, at least what she could see of it. "I think that's Franz and John Fuller up there."

"Franz came here with Laszlo just before he died. I was really impressed because I assumed they climbed the rocks, but since there's an easier trail, that's probably what they took. I'm surprised Franz would come again, but John probably convinced him to go. It's good he's getting out."

"It's very good."

We walked the level part, and shortly after the trail grew steep, I found a bench a short distance from the pathway, a bench shaded by bushes. "This is the spot for me. I'll be here reading when you get back."

Andrea forged ahead, and I sat down to wait for her. I was immediately so engrossed in my book that I didn't notice

Klaus and Karla Becker till they were practically upon me. "Oh, hello! Are you planning to hike to the top?"

"Yes," Klaus said, and Karla smiled and nodded. They walked right on without stopping to chat. I was going to tell them that Andrea was ahead of them, but I didn't want to be shouting at their backs.

I went back to my book, thinking that Klaus, being somewhat paunchy and not looking as if he's in the best shape, might find the walk strenuous. Then I couldn't help thinking that if he had been the one responsible for Laszlo's overdose of digitalis, it would be some sort of justice if he had a heart attack on the way up. Just as I was thinking this, the girls came trailing along behind them. They were in shorts and sneakers, and they were giggling and chatting with each other in German. I heard Nicole mention Laszlo, and the two of them howled with laughter. They were so preoccupied they never noticed me. I had no idea what they were saying, but the mention of the murdered man and their reaction sent a chill up my back. Could they have joined forces to commit murder?

Now if Erika and the sisters showed up, all of Stefan's family and friends would be on the rocks. The idea conjured up all kinds of possibilities, since there probably was a murderer among them. I wondered if there was an area at the top where someone could lose their footing and fall to their death.

Then, as if on cue, the sisters came along. They were speaking in German as well, and I heard both of them say Laszlo's name as they approached. Their conversation sounded dead serious, as opposed to that of Amalie and Nicole. They noticed me, and both looked as if they wished they hadn't mentioned the murdered man. "Out for a hike, I see," I said, trying to sound cheerful, as if I'd been busy reading and was oblivious to their conversation.

"We're going to the top," Claudia said, and they hurried past me.

I had been reading for what seemed like hours when I heard voices and realized some of the hikers were coming back down. It turned out all of them were coming down, chatting and cheerful as can be. Franz seemed to have enjoyed the outing, and he stopped and spoke to me.

"How was it at the top?" I asked.

"It's a wonderful view up there. There's a convenient viewing pavilion. You should try it sometime."

"I'm sure Andrea took pictures. I'll check out her camera and see the view that way."

Andrea came along and suggested everyone return to the hotel for coffee and cake, and they all agreed this was a good idea. Andrea called Ivy, and she had a pot ready when we got there. The girls took three pieces of cake and went off to find David, and the men brought chairs from the kitchen so we all could sit around the fireplace. Even when there was no fire, it was the logical gathering place. Ivy could join us and still keep an eye on the desk.

Everyone seemed to be having such a good time, eating cake and chatting about the trek up Seneca Rocks, that you'd never have known a murder had been committed in our midst. Then it occurred to me that the rest of them didn't know yet that it had been murder. They were all assuming it had been a simple heart attack. All but one, possibly.

We were just finishing and everyone was starting to disperse when the door opened and Ward and Willard walked in, both in uniform. "If you'll all go to your rooms, we need statements from all of you. We'll call on you when we're ready."

Franz looked upset. "What's this about?"

"Laszlo Novacek's death."

"Then you're saying . . . what are you saying?"

"What we're saying right now is that we need statements from everyone who was in the hotel on the night of Mr. Novacek's death. We also need to talk to Mr. Fuller."

The sheriff wasn't a man to be argued with; he had that kind of presence, so we all quietly went to our rooms. Now the whole group would be wondering if it really was a simple heart attack, and thinking it probably wasn't.

"This was no surprise, after what Willard told us," I whispered.

"No surprise at all. The only surprise is that they didn't do it sooner. Maybe they were waiting for everyone to be here. Erika hasn't come in yet."

"Maybe they figured they'd never find a time when everyone was here, unless they came very early or late. I suppose Erika will be here by the time they get through questioning the rest of us. She probably went shopping."

It was quite some time before we heard a knock on our door. They were leaving us till last, I figured, because the others were more likely to compare stories and, if they were guilty, come up with an alibi. Besides, neither of us had a motive for murder.

Willard was at the door. "If you'll come with me, Ms. Williamson . . . Kathleen, the sheriff will talk to Andrea upstairs."

Willard and I sat by the fireplace, which was blazing by now. Asbury must have come in and started it. I told Willard everything I could remember from the time we arrived at the Alpenhof till the morning after Laszlo's death.

He had a couple of questions for me: "Have you seen anything since you've been here that seemed out of the ordinary?" and I couldn't think of anything. Then he said, "I have to ask this: Did Stefan or Maggie ever indicate to you that Stefan expected to inherit a great deal of money from Laszlo Novacek?"

Willard had a tape recorder going, and also was taking notes. "Never!" I answered emphatically for the benefit of the recorder. "Maggie would have told me if she had known of such a thing."

He turned off the recorder. "Thanks, Kathleen. We really appreciate your cooperation."

Then I remembered talking with Maggie in the restroom at the lodge restaurant on the first night we all ate together. I was embarrassed to admit I had been so nosy, but if it meant diverting suspicion from Maggie and Stefan, I had to do it. "There's something more I thought of."

I had hoped he wouldn't, but Willard turned the tape recorder back on. "Go ahead."

"I asked Maggie if Laszlo had money because of the luxurious Cadillac he had rented. She said he had a lot of money. Then I asked whether she knew who would inherit all that money when he was gone, and she said, 'We don't know.'

She went on to add, jokingly, that he probably would be leaving it to a home for ageing Casanovas."

Willard looked puzzled. "Why would she say that?"

"Apparently Laszlo was quite a ladies' man."

He nodded and turned off the recorder, much to my relief. "You still haven't found the kids, I take it."

"Nothing. They seem to have fallen off the face of the Earth. I'll let you know right away if we hear anything, don't worry."

"Has the sheriff made sense of the checkbook entry showing a payment from Laszlo to Klaus Becker?" After I said this, I wondered whether the sheriff had discussed the checkbook with Willard.

He obviously had. "I'm sure he's questioning Mr. Becker about that this evening. It's not a whole lot of money, so I doubt it has any great significance."

"How was your evening with Hadley at that nice restaurant near Elkins?" I couldn't remember the name of it.

He smiled and seemed to relax. "It was wonderful. There's one thing that concerns me, though. She's a criminology major, and it would be great if we could work together, but I don't know if the sheriff would hire her if we have a thing going."

"I have a feeling the sheriff might be a tad old-fashioned, too, and wouldn't want to put a woman in a dangerous job. I remember that in January, Andrea told me the only woman employee there was the dispatcher."

Willard just smiled. He had turned the tape recorder off earlier, but he still didn't want to comment on whether he thought the sheriff was old-fashioned.

"Are you through now? Are Andrea and I the last?"

"I think Mrs. Novacek has now come home. We still need to talk to her."

"Have you talked to Juliet Gorsky?"

"Yes, she was in her room, and the sheriff talked to her."

"I'll go back to our room, then, and let you get on with it."

"Thanks again, Kathleen. As usual, it's been good talking to you."

I had been in our room only a few minutes when Andrea came in. "Did Ward ask you about Maggie and Stefan, and whether they knew Stefan would inherit a fortune when Laszlo died?"

"Yes, he did. I suppose everyone's a suspect at this point."

"But they weren't even here when Laszlo died. The fact that there was no cup in his room ought to clear them. Even if they had put foxglove in his teabags, they wouldn't have been here to remove the cup."

"I know, but we can't solve anything tonight. Let's drive to that little store down the road and pick up a sandwich. We can bring it back here and eat it."

#

We ate the sandwiches in front of the fire, accompanied by drinks from the machine by the ice dispenser. Back in our room, Andrea sat down on the bed and started taking off her hiking boots. "This case reminds me of *Murder on the Orient Express.*"

"The Agatha Christie book? Why is that?

"There are so many people who had a motive, including Stefan and Maggie."

"Surely you're not serious about Stefan and Maggie."

"I don't think seriously that Maggie or Stefan could have committed murder, but to an objective observer, they have just as much motive as anyone else here. Maybe more. I was thinking of all the folks in the hotel and their motives, and I couldn't help thinking of that particular mystery novel."

"I suppose it's possible that the entire group got together and planned his death. Everyone but Maggie and Stefan, that is."

Andrea got up and headed for the bathroom. "Anyway, I'm taking a shower and going to bed. That hike made me tired—a good kind of tired."

I almost wished I was a good kind of tired too, but instead I went to bed and pored over the question of whether the sheriff was actually suspicious of either Maggie or Stefan. Finally, I got up at two o'clock and went to the bathroom, then wandered to the window and pulled back the curtain. There on the bench were two people, and though the moon wasn't as bright tonight, I knew it had to be David and Nicole. They were just sitting there talking—harmless enough, and probably typical of teenagers these days. I went back to bed and drifted off to dream my usual turbulent dreams of someone stalking hotel guests.

#

We both woke up early, Andrea looking rested and radiant, while I looked like something left over from a wild all-night party. We were dressed and ready to go to the lobby when we heard the scream this time, and my stomach tightened into a hard little ball. "Good God, what now?"

"That's what I'm going to find out," Andrea said as she rushed out of the room.

CHAPTER SEVEN

Hadley was pale and sobbing hysterically. "So much blood," she kept saying. Andrea took her by the arm, and she said, "It's Mr. Fuller."

My first thought, which was totally inappropriate, was that this woman wasn't equipped to work in the field of criminology. My second was, why does she keep going into rooms that are occupied, even if it's by the dead? Andrea had taken her cell phone from her pocket and was calling someone. I was sure it was the sheriff.

We heard sirens right away, and a deputy I didn't recognize came through the entrance. He walked to the desk, where Ivy said, "It seems to be Mr. Fuller, from what I can understand from Hadley. He's in Room Six." She pointed down the hallway.

We were still hearing sirens, and soon Willard walked in, followed by Ward. Both were looking grim, as if they'd had about enough of this nonsense. They followed the first deputy down the hallway. Franz and Erika came into the lobby, and pretty soon the Beckers were there, too.

"What's happened now?" Franz asked.

"It's John Fuller. We don't know for sure what the situation is."

Ivy motioned for me, and I knew before she said anything that she wanted me to make coffee. "Would you like me to make coffee?"

"Please. Use the big pot."

I went to the kitchen and took the thirty-cup pot from the shelf where Ivy kept it, filled it, and started it perking. There was nothing left but cake, and there wasn't enough for everyone, so the group would have to be satisfied with coffee till they could go somewhere and have breakfast.

By the time I returned to the lobby, Harvey Davis, the medical examiner, had arrived and was heading back to Room

Six. That wing of the hotel has six rooms, and from what I could figure, the Beckers were in Room One, and their girls were across from them in Room Two. I guess Asbury had put John Fuller as far as possible from them, with an empty room between, in case they were noisy. Little did he know that Nicole spent most of her time outside, hanging out with David, and Amalie was quiet as a dormouse.

By this time everyone registered at the hotel was in the lobby, waiting around for coffee and waiting to see what had happened to John Fuller. The sheriff came out right away. "I don't want anyone to leave the hotel till we've had a chance to talk to each of you. Please stay here in the lobby until you're called. I've asked a deputy to bring in some biscuits and sweet rolls so you can have something to eat, because this is going to take some time."

Franz spoke up. "What's happened to John?"

"Mr. Fuller is deceased."

"What happened? How?"

"I can't discuss that right now. If you'll come with me, Mr. Novacek, well talk first, and Willard can talk to Mrs. Novacek. Then the two of you can leave if you need to go somewhere." They went upstairs to a sitting area in the hallway that led back from the stairs and overlooked the backyard of the hotel. Willard and Erika went to the kitchen and sat at a table in the far corner. I went to the kitchen, said, "Excuse me," and filled a tray with coffee cups. I couldn't hear what Willard and Erika were saying, and they didn't object to my being there.

I added a jar of creamer and some packets of sweetener to the tray and carried it to the table in front of the fireplace. The deputy must have arrived; three boxes of biscuits and rolls sat on the table also. Everyone gathered around and helped themselves, and I took coffee to Ivy. She didn't want anything to eat at the moment.

All this time I'd been thinking about seeing David and Nicole outside our window at two o'clock and feeling uncomfortable about mentioning it to Willard or Ward. There really was no need to feel uncomfortable; they were just kids having a good time chatting in the middle of the night. Their being out there couldn't have any bearing on the case.

I guess what made me reluctant to talk about it was the idea that David and Nicole might swear they were sound asleep in bed, and my statement would prove this to be untrue. I hadn't bothered to tell Andrea this morning that I had seen them again. We'd hardly had time to talk before Hadley screamed.

Andrea and I were the last to be interviewed, and this time Ward asked me to go upstairs with him while Andrea talked with Willard in the kitchen. I told Ward about going to Seneca Rocks and seeing so many of our group there, about hearing Laszlo's name mentioned, and then returning to the hotel for coffee and cake. He asked me for specifics about the hike, and I had to admit I sat on a bench and read while the rest, and I named them, went to the top. I told him about going out for sandwiches after talking with Willard and him, and finally, reluctantly, I told him about getting up in the middle of the night and seeing two people at the picnic table.

I explained that we had seen David and Nicole there a week ago, when there was bright moonlight, and that I assumed it was them again. Talking about the moon, I couldn't help but remember that we were now at the waning halfmoon, a time of turmoil and trouble. I still couldn't fathom the puzzle of Laszlo's death on the night of the full moon.

I explained that we got up this morning and got dressed just before hearing Hadley scream. I hoped I hadn't created a problem for David. "Can I ask you something?"

He smiled, just faintly. "You can ask. I can't promise that I can answer."

"Did David tell you about being out last night?"

Ward looked as if he couldn't decide whether to answer, but finally said, "Yes, he did. I was surprised and pleased that he talked so freely about what he was doing."

"I'm surprised and pleased, too. Thank you." I went back to the lobby, feeling relieved that I hadn't contradicted David's statement.

Andrea was already there. "Would you like some breakfast, or is it too late for breakfast?"

"I ate two biscuits, so I'm not awfully hungry at the moment. I was thinking we might go over to the restaurant Willard mentioned for lunch. Do you remember the name of it?"

"The Cheat River Inn. They may not be open for lunch. Maggie gave me the key to her room so I could use her computer if I wanted to. Let's go up, and I'll see if they have a website."

"How do you suppose John Fuller died? Hadley kept mentioning blood, so I wonder if he was stabbed. I'd think we would have heard a shot."

"He probably was stabbed, and I'm sure we can count on learning about it eventually."

Andrea, mysterious as usual, probably was informed by Willard and was reluctant to talk about it. "Did Willard say anything?"

"No, he didn't. I'm just guessing, like you are."

"And how do you suppose the killer gets into the rooms? Do people leave their doors unlocked at night?"

"I don't know, but Ivy has spare keys at the desk, and there's no one on the desk after ten. I don't imagine they've taken any precaution to secure the keys, but I'd think they would now."

By this time we were upstairs and Andrea was unlocking Maggie's door. She walked in and froze in front of the computer. "Someone's been in here. The computer's on, and Maggie never leaves it on."

It didn't look on to me—the screen was black, but then I noticed a light in the big rectangular box beside the screen. "Are you sure? She might have been distracted by the wedding and forgot to turn it off."

"I don't think so. She told me before the wedding that the computer was off, and she told me to use it whenever I wanted." Andrea took her cell phone from her pocket and started punching buttons.

"Who are you calling?" I asked, but she started talking on the phone before she had a chance to answer. She was telling the person on the other end about the computer being on, so I assumed it was Ward Sterling.

She turned the phone off. "He's still down in John Fuller's room, and he's asked a deputy who's tech-savvy to come to the hotel to see what they can figure out. Don't touch anything on the way out. We'll lock up till they get here."

"Do you suppose someone was being nosy and tried to figure out where the kids went on their honeymoon?" I asked.

"That was my first thought. Then I wondered whether they were researching digitalis. Unless it was one of these objectives, why would anyone want to use Maggie's computer, since nearly everyone has one of their own. I can't help wondering whether it was the same person who committed the murders. That person may have found the spare keys at the registration desk and used them to get into all three rooms."

We went to the lobby and had more coffee till a deputy who looked about fifteen arrived. Ward came down the hallway from John Fuller's room, and we followed him and the deputy upstairs—I think Andrea was hoping to get a look at what the young man would do on the computer, or possibly she already knew. The first thing they did was dust everything for fingerprints, but everything had been wiped clean. Not something Maggie would have done, of course, and I was sure the sheriff would agree with this also.

The young man worked on the computer for a few minutes and reported to Ward that someone had been searching various sites related to foxglove and digitalis. He was murmuring so I could barely hear him, and I suppose he wasn't sure Andrea and I should hear what he was saying. No emails had been sent since the morning of the wedding, and these were sent by Maggie giving details of the wedding to faraway friends.

"When was the research done," Ward asked.

"Thursday afternoon before the wedding."

I was both worried and angry that Maggie's computer had been used to research the poison that killed Laszlo. "Maggie and Stefan were in Parsons to see about the flowers for the wedding that Thursday afternoon," I said. "That was the day we arrived, and they were gone for quite a while that afternoon."

Neither of the men appeared to pay any attention to me; they were busy checking things on the screen. Finally the deputy shut the computer down and began unplugging what seemed to be dozens of wires behind it. He picked up the rectangular box beside the screen and walked out with it.

Andrea looked frustrated because the computer was being taken away, but she didn't say anything about it. Instead, she said, "If that research was done Thursday afternoon, then someone must have been in here again after Maggie and Stefan left, because she distinctly told me she turned the computer off on the night of the wedding."

Ward turned and looked at her. "It's possible she was confused. After all, it was the night of her wedding."

"The fact that all fingerprints in the area were wiped off indicates that someone was in the room, don't you think?" Andrea asked. "Maggie's prints should have been on there if she used it and then simply forgot to turn it off."

"That's the assumption we'd normally make," Ward said.

The sheriff wasn't committing himself to anything. What a pair he and Andrea would make, if only they'd get together. Both were so hesitant to jump to conclusions, while I, on the other hand, jumped to them all the time.

"Maybe I can use the computer at the desk. We wanted to look up the Cheat River Inn to see if they're open for lunch."

Ward shook his head. "Don't bother. They're only open for supper. If I can work out a free evening, I'd like to take you." He looked at me. "Both of you."

I hated the idea of being an afterthought, but I didn't know what to say, so I said nothing for a change.

"We'd enjoy that," Andrea said, "especially since we don't know the way, and Willard said it's not right in town."

"I'll let you know when I can get an evening free. With two murders to unravel, I'm not sure when that'll be."

"We'll look forward to it when the current situation is resolved."

Ward now was calling them both murders, so there was no doubt about the deaths of the two hotel guests. I felt a certain grim satisfaction in knowing that much, at least. Andrea locked Maggie's room, and we went downstairs.

"I'm afraid someone's trying to frame Maggie for Laszlo's murder," I said. "The person who researched the poison obviously knew how to do research, so you'd think they'd have a computer of their own. I just hope Ward heard what I said about Maggie and Stefan being in Parsons that afternoon."

"If he didn't, I'll make a point of telling him again. I wasn't able to see what time the research was done, so we'll have to hope it was the same time that the kids were in that flower shop. And since a friend of theirs is doing the flowers, I'm sure she'll remember their being there."

We drank more coffee and debated about how to spend the day. It was almost noon when Erika came down the hallway. "Would you two like to go to lunch? My husband isn't feeling well again, with the news of John's death. He wants to stay in, and says he doesn't want anything to eat."

"Would you like to go back to The Sawmill?" Andrea asked. "We were thinking of going to Davis and having lunch, and then looking around in the shops there."

"I'd prefer the Blackwater Lodge, if it's all the same to you. I thought it was such a delightful place when we were there before. It's so close to Davis, we could still go shopping."

I couldn't help wondering why she thought it was such a delightful place, when that's where the sisters got angry and walked out on her. "I'm going to ask Ivy if she could get free to go with us."

"Asbury and David are all tied up with mowing and trimming the lawn today, so I can't leave the desk. Besides, with all that's going on here, I think I need to stay. I'm afraid I'm in trouble."

"What's wrong?"

"The spare keys have disappeared. I don't know when it happened, because I haven't needed any of them in a couple of weeks. I only open the bottom drawer and get one out when a guest misplaces his key. The sheriff asked about keys this morning, and I opened the drawer to show him. There was nothing there."

"They can't blame you. I suppose they've always been kept in that drawer, and you had no reason to check on them, especially with all that's been going on around here."

"I'm not sure they see it that way, now that we've had two murders."

"I suppose Hadley has a set, too."

"Yes, and when she's done, she locks them in the supply room off the laundry. She carries the key to that room with her. She hasn't said anything about keys being missing. It's just the spare set we kept here at the desk."

"I'm sorry you can't go with us. Can we bring you something?"

"Thanks, but Asbury will stop long enough to relieve me for lunch. The rest of you go and have a good time."

I debated on the way to the Blackwater Lodge about whether to tell Andrea about the missing keys in front of Erika, but decided there was no reason not to. After we had ordered—salads, of course, since I didn't want to eat more than Erika—I said, "Ivy was telling me that the spare set of keys to the hotel rooms have disappeared."

"When did this happen?"

"She's not sure. She hadn't opened the drawer where they're kept for about two weeks. She only goes into that drawer when someone loses a key, and that hasn't happened lately."

Erika grimaced. "You mean the madman who's already killed two people has keys to all our rooms? I'm going to have to talk to Stefan about the lax security at the hotel. And I'm going to get one of those chairs from the kitchen and put the back under our doorknob. Do you know how to do that?"

Andrea nodded. "I know, but I don't think the rest of us are in any danger. There must have been some connection between Laszlo and John Fuller that resulted in both their deaths. Did they have a current business proposition underway, as far as you know?"

Erika shook her head. "I knew nothing about their business. Franz didn't either. He's always too busy with embassy affairs to get involved with Laszlo's complicated business dealings, and we saw John on a social level at times, maybe once a month, but he never talked business. It was always the latest theater or opera event, or the latest book he was reading. I always had the impression he was glad to have someone to talk to outside of business."

"Was he married?" I asked.

"Divorced. He married young, then divorced in a few years. He never remarried. I think his ex-wife is living in Austria and is remarried. She'd have no reason to harm him, and didn't even know Laszlo."

"We haven't seen much of Claudia and Agnes since we all hiked up Seneca Rocks. I wonder what they're doing lately," Andrea said.

"I have no idea," Erika said. "I've always loved Agnes. She was Stefan's nanny till he was almost too old to have a nanny. We always liked her so much. Claudia's a different story. I don't know if you know this, but Agnes was engaged to Laszlo at one time. She's such a sweet and naïve person, she didn't realize Claudia was having an affair with him at the same time."

"And yet they're on friendly terms now," Andrea said.

"Agnes came upon Claudia and Laszlo in a compromising situation, and the sisters were estranged for years. Claudia managed to wheedle her way back into Agnes' affection and to turn her totally against Laszlo. Heaven knows, she had reason enough to hate him anyway."

Trying to figure out how to fish for more information without appearing too obvious, I said, "They both must be terribly temperamental, the way they stomped out of here the other day."

Erika laughed. "You're so right. They brought up the subject of Laszlo, and all I said was that I thought he'd always been a little in love with me. Their reaction makes me wonder if they both have feelings for him still. Even Agnes, even-tempered as she is, was somewhat miffed."

I was stunned that she divulged this, and I'm sure Andrea was, too. As a matter of fact, I was so stunned that I didn't know what to say next. Andrea did, though. "Were you and Laszlo ever engaged?"

"He asked me to marry him at one time, but when I met Franz, I fell in love with him. Laszlo took it well, and we all stayed on good terms."

So European, I thought. I couldn't imagine people staying on good terms under those conditions. Or maybe the terms weren't as good as Erika would like us to believe.

The waitress came with our food, and we concentrated on that for a while. Then I was back to mulling over what Erika had said, and wondering if a motive for murder was lurking there.

#

We spent the afternoon browsing in shops but buying very little. At four, we went back to Blackwater Lodge for apple pie and coffee, which was welcome after all the walking we did while shopping. We had just finished our pie and were waiting for a second cup of coffee when Claudia and Agnes walked in. They didn't look at us. "Speak of the devil," I whispered.

Andrea frowned at me; Erika giggled. The sisters pointed to a table as far from us as possible, and the hostess led them there. "It looks like alliances are being formed," I said.

"I'll get a chance to talk to them at the lodge," Andrea said. "They have no reason to be upset with any of us, including Erika."

We finished our second cup of coffee and went back to the Alpenhof, where Asbury had already started a fire in the fireplace. He was behind the desk. Andrea and I went over to talk to him, while Erika went on to their room. "We haven't seen you lately, Asbury," I said.

"Good afternoon. Ivy went to the store. She has a pot of navy beans cooking, and she's gonna make some cornbread. We wondered if you'd like to come over and eat with us this evening."

"I'd love it," Andrea said.

I nodded in agreement. "We both live alone in Pine Summit, and neither of us cooks much. It'll be a real treat to have a cornbread and bean supper."

"Come over at six. This is one night when Hadley fills in for us on the desk here during suppertime. She does that two nights a week, so we can sit down together with David and have a meal. I'll tell Ivy you're coming, so she can set the places."

We went to our room and showered, then lay down for a quick nap before suppertime. After two cups of coffee, I just wasn't sleepy, however. "I'm wondering again if one of the sisters killed Laszlo, after what Erika said today about why they were upset with her. What do you think?"

Andrea turned toward me. "They have a motive of sorts, but I'm not sure it's strong enough for murder. And there's this—if the same person killed John Fuller, then what reason would the sisters have for killing him?"

"I don't know. I wonder if they even knew him. Of course, they could have killed him to make it look like someone who had something against both of them did it."

Andrea nodded. "That doesn't sound likely, but I suppose anything is possible at this stage of the game. I can't help wondering if John was involved in the same venture where Klaus lost all his money. That might explain a lot if we could find out."

"I don't know how we'd ever check on that, and John certainly isn't around to tell us, is he."

"That's for sure."

"What do you think about Franz?" I murmured.

"He seems genuinely disturbed about Laszlo's death. And I don't suppose he'd have a motive to kill his brother."

I sat up and thought about this for a moment. "Unless he discovered Erika was having an affair with Laszlo."

"Oh, horrors! I'd hate to think Stefan's parents are an adulteress and a murderer. We've just acquired him as a nephew-in-law."

I always manage to think up wild theories in any situation, and I love to bounce them off Andrea. "I've been wondering if Nicole could have talked David into killing both those people."

"More horrors! I don't think David could be talked into such a thing. I admit, Nicole's college money disappeared because of Laszlo, but at her age, I don't think she'd take it that seriously."

"She's by far the more aggressive of the two girls. On the other hand, Amalie had her heart set on going to Heidelberg, according to Maggie, and she's been forced to attend some small college in Berlin."

"I've no doubt the sheriff will solve this case before long. Then we'll be able to go to the Cheat River Inn. I'm looking forward to that."

I sighed. "I'm going to have a headache that night."

"Why on earth do you say that?"

"I think Ward wants some time alone with you, and he only invited me to be polite."

"You're mistaken, and I'll insist you go with us."

"Good heavens! It's a quarter till six. We'd better get ready."

We put on jeans and sweaters and went to the lobby. Hadley was already at the desk. "How are you doing?" I asked.

"I think I've recovered somewhat from the shock of finding two bodies. I haven't told Willard yet, but I think I'm changing my major from criminology to hospitality management. I talked to my advisor this morning, and she agreed it might be a good idea, considering my reaction to the events here."

"With all the tourism in this area, that would be a good major," I said.

"I do have a son to raise, and getting into a dangerous profession probably wouldn't be the wisest choice anyway. Seeing those bodies brought this home to me."

"We'd better go," Andrea said. "We're going over to eat with Ivy and Asbury," she explained to Hadley.

"That's nice. I understand Ivy's a good cook."

We went through the kitchen and out the back door. We'd never been in the small house where Asbury and his family lived, and I was curious. We entered into a living room that had a couch and a couple of armchairs grouped around a television set. To the left was a hallway which probably led to bedrooms and a bathroom—the house was too small to have more than one bath. On the right was the kitchen with an adjacent small dining area. A table was set up there, with a tablecloth, plates, and silverware already in place. As far as we could see, everything was immaculate, but that was no surprise. Ivy always comes across as a woman who knows how to run a proper household.

She came from the kitchen to greet us. "I'm so glad you could come. Be a change for you, from all the highfalutin food in the restaurants around here. Not that I haven't enjoyed going to those restaurants with you, but it's good to get back to the basics now and then"

"Amen!" I said. "Is there anything we can do to help?"

"No, everything's ready. Asbury! David!"

They both appeared from the other side of the house.

"Did you wash your hands?"

They both disappeared again, back to what must be the bathroom.

Ivy shook her head. "They just never grow up."

Ivy had dipped up a large serving bowl of navy beans, and she put a platter of cornbread squares on the table. David brought a bowl of coleslaw from the refrigerator, and we all sat down together. I split a piece of cornbread on my plate and poured the soupy beans over it, with coleslaw on the side. "Heaven," was all I could say before I started eating.

We were all too busy enjoying Ivy's wonderful food to say much, but when we were through, she brought coffee—decaf, she said—and a carrot cake. "May I be excused," David said.

"He's going to the movies over in Elkins tonight with Jeremy and Nicole. She's driving her father's rental car," Ivy said.

I set my coffee cup on the saucer. "You're going all the way to Elkins? Why not Davis?"

"There's no theater in Davis."

"Amalie isn't going with you, too?"

"She thinks we're a bunch of young kids. She doesn't want to hang out with us."

"You don't want to stay and have cake first?" Ivy asked.

"I'll have some when I get back." He rushed out the door.

I must say, I was somewhat concerned about his going off with Nicole, driving on strange mountain roads in the dark. Ivy and Asbury didn't look all that pleased with it, either, but none of us said anything for a while.

"Your cake is delicious," Andrea said, "and so was everything else. We really appreciate your inviting us."

"We're just glad you could come," Asbury said. He looked like he was debating about what to say next, but finally said, "I hope you're locking your door up tight at night. With a murderer running loose on the place, we can't be too careful."

"We definitely are," Andrea said. "I think the hotel needs a security review when the kids get back. This is such a beautiful and quiet area, you wouldn't think such violence could happen here."

We finished our cake and coffee and helped Ivy with washing up. We knew she had to get back to the desk to relieve Hadley, so we excused ourselves and started back to the hotel.

"Did you see that?" Andrea asked as we were crossing the lawn.

Without waiting for me to answer, she started running toward the back door. I looked at the hotel and saw a flash of light in the one of the second-floor rooms, and I guessed Andrea knew it was the one Laszlo had occupied. Someone was up there with a flashlight. There's no way I could run, but I started after Andrea as fast I could walk, knowing she was on her way to Laszlo's room and a murderer.

As I went through the kitchen and past the closed door of the laundry room, I could hear a dryer running. I didn't take time to give it any thought, but followed Andrea into the lobby and up the stairs. She was standing at the door to Room Twelve. It was dark and quiet inside.

Andrea turned on the light. "Someone's looking for something up here, but whatever they're looking for, I don't think it's here. We searched everything thoroughly with Ward the other evening."

We went back downstairs, where Hadley was looking at us with a puzzled expression on her face. "We saw a light upstairs and wondered what was going on," Andrea said. "Did you see anyone from down on this floor go up the stairs?"

"No one went up there, unless it was during the few minutes when I went to Mr. Novacek's room to get him for a phone call."

"I heard a dryer running in the laundry room when I came through," I said.

Andrea immediately headed back that way, with me following. She opened the door to the laundry, and Karla Becker was leaning on a dryer, looking at a magazine.

"We were thinking of doing a load of laundry, too," Andrea said.

Karla smiled and nodded. "We had too many dirty clothes building up."

I couldn't help thinking that for a family of four, one dryer-full wouldn't do it. Maybe she was washing the bloody clothes she wore when stabbing John Fuller. Or maybe she was washing those of her husband.

Back in the lobby, we sat down by the fire. "She could have been the one upstairs, and if she heard us coming, she could have gone down the hallway to the attic stairs, and from there, down to the laundry room."

Andrea nodded. "I thought of that, but I didn't see a flashlight. It's possible she hid it on the stairs to the attic and planned to hide it in the dry clothes when they were through. I'm going to toss a few things in the washer and hang out in there till she leaves. If there's a flashlight in the stairwell, she won't have a chance to get it without my seeing her."

We rushed back to our room and Andrea grabbed our trash bag full of dirty clothes from the closet floor. When we got back to the lobby, Ivy was back behind the desk. "We're going to do a load of laundry," Andrea said as we passed through.

"Help yourself."

Karla was still in the laundry room when we got there. We started our things in a washer, then tried to make small talk with Karla till her dryer stopped. When it did, she painstakingly took everything out and began folding it on a table in the corner. It wasn't a big load—just enough to include clothes worn during a bloody murder and a few more things to take away suspicion.

She finally finished folding, and Andrea said, "Would you like a drink from the machine outside?"

She smiled and nodded. "Yes, please. A Coke."

We walked with her to the machine and picked out our drinks, and when Karla had hers, she went back to the laundry, gathered up her clothes, said goodnight, and headed for her room.

"Drat!" Andrea said. "I was hoping to get that can with her fingerprints on it. Then if we find the flashlight, fingerprints on both could be compared."

"Maybe they could check the dryer she was using, and if prints there matched the flashlight . . ."

"There are probably a lot of prints on the dryer, and if one of them did match the ones on the flashlight, we still wouldn't know whose it was. Of course, we haven't found a flashlight yet. Let's go look."

We went to the laundry room and opened the door to the attic stairs. Andrea took her key chain from her pocket and turned on a small but very effective LED flashlight. We saw nothing on the stairs, so Andrea went around and looked under them. There, in a back corner, she found a small flashlight. She picked it up gingerly by the rim around the bulb. "Get a zipper bag from the kitchen, please, and we'll give this to Ward."

As soon as she had the flashlight secured in the bag, she dialed the sheriff and explained what had happened. He said he'd be by to pick up the flashlight in an hour—he had news for us, anyway. We finished the laundry before he got there, wondering what his news could be, and hoping it wasn't about Maggie and Stefan.

By the time we were through and had put our clothes in the drawers of our chest, Ivy had left the desk. Everything at the Alpenhof shuts down at ten, and guests coming back late push a buzzer at the door. It sounds in Stefan's room, and he comes down and lets them in. He has a phone in his room, too, an extension of the hotel number. I assume guests have been instructed to dial Asbury's number during Stefan's absence. Nobody told us anything, but we're more like family than guests here. Also, we're never out after ten.

It occurred to me for the first time to wonder about the kids sitting on the picnic table in the middle of the night. David probably had a key to their house and could get in with no trouble. Nicole may have climbed out a window and came back into her room the same way, or possibly she knocked on a window and Amalie got up and let her in.

We sat in the lobby to wait for the sheriff and finally heard a knock on the door. Andrea turned the deadbolt and opened it. It wasn't the sheriff, but Nicole, back from the movie. "How was the movie?" I asked.

"Fine." She flounced on down the hall and into her room.

"At least we know she wasn't the one with the flashlight," I said.

Andrea just looked thoughtful at this remark, always reserving judgment, as usual. As far as she's concerned, anything is possible until proven otherwise. Then my thoughts were interrupted by another knock. "This has to be the sheriff," and it was.

"Let's sit down a minute," he said, and took off his jacket and laid it across the back of the couch. "I just wanted to let you know we've finally located Maggie and Stefan. They're down on the Blue Ridge Parkway, and they said they'd come on home tomorrow. They had car trouble in White Sulphur Springs, so they left the Volvo in a shop and rented a car. They have to go by and pick up her car and return the rental car, but they should be able to make it in a day."

We didn't want him to know Willard had blabbed about the Volvo being located and so forth, so we didn't say anything. I couldn't help feeling a little relieved that they'd been found, even though we wanted them to enjoy their honeymoon. At least they'd had a week. It would be wonderful to see them again, especially in these nerve-wracking times. Knowing they'd be here to make decisions about the hotel and tighten up security was comforting.

Andrea went to our room and got the bagged flashlight and gave it to the sheriff, and we told him good night and turned the deadbolt behind him. Back in our room, Andrea checked her cell phone, which was plugged into the charger on the chest. "There's a call from Maggie on here." She listened, then played it over for me.

"Hi, Andrea and Kathleen. A deputy stopped us near Buena Vista and gave us the news about what's been happening at the hotel. Stefan is devastated about his uncle's death. They always had a special relationship. Sorry we weren't there to help handle all this. We hope to see you tomorrow. Love you. Bye."

I turned the phone off and put it back on the charger. "Much as I wanted them to enjoy two wonderful weeks, I'm glad they're coming home."

"I am, too. It'll be reassuring to have them here."

The notion that Andrea needed reassurance about anything was news to me; she's always been so self-reliant. I took the chair we had brought from the kitchen and jammed it under the door handle and then made sure the door was locked.

CHAPTER EIGHT

Claudia and Agnes were drinking coffee in the lobby when we came from our room. "Good morning," I said, and they smiled and said, "Good morning," too. I wondered whether Andrea talked to them, since they were so friendly.

Andrea came back from the kitchen with coffee for both of us. "What are you two doing for breakfast?"

"We were thinking of going over to the lodge, then going for a hike at Cathedral State Park," Claudia said. "Would you like to join us?"

"We'll join you for breakfast. We just visited Cathedral State Park a few days ago, and we have other plans for today." Andrea looked at me for confirmation, and I nodded.

We took off for the Canaan Lodge in separate cars. "I want to go back to the hotel after we eat and look through Laszlo's room again. There must be something there that someone's looking for. It's possible they found it last night, but if they didn't, I'm going to find it today if I have to tear the place apart."

We arrived at the lodge at the same time as the sisters and walked into the restaurant together. A waitress brought menus and water, and we all ordered coffee. "Who went to Cathedral State Park with you when you went there the other day?" Agnes asked.

"Just the two of us and Erika. We did a lot of walking and took many photos. It's a beautiful park."

"I'm surprised Erika would go somewhere like that. She spends most of her time shopping, it seems," Claudia said.

Agnes put her hand on Claudia's arm, as if to restrain her. "I love Erika. I worked for them for years when Stefan was young, and of course I love Stefan, too."

Claudia shrugged. "It seems to me that there were problems in their household back then, and probably are today."

The waitress brought coffee and took our orders, and Andrea added half and half to hers and looked directly at Claudia. "Erika is Maggie's mother-in-law now, so I don't think it's appropriate to discuss her when she isn't present. Actually, I don't think it would be right to discuss her even if she weren't Maggie's mother-in-law. Unless we're talking about how attractive she is, or how bright."

Darn! I thought we were on the brink of some juicy revelation, and Andrea squelches it. She's fascinated by a mystery and would be glad to hear anything related to the deaths at the hotel, but she has no use for gossip. I, on the other hand, have been known to indulge. I decided it would be appropriate to say something complimentary about Erika. "She looked stunning in that red dress she had on the other day at the Blackwater Lodge. She's a very attractive woman."

"Yes, she is," Agnes said. "I felt bad about the way we walked out on her. It was just the result of the tension we've all been feeling lately, and I apologized to her later."

Claudia sniffed but didn't say anything, looking like apologizing was the last thing she'd think of doing. "You were ahead of us, Andrea. How did the Beckers make it to the top at Seneca Rocks?"

At this point in the conversation, I don't think Andrea would have told Claudia if Klaus Becker had collapsed from exhaustion and died on the spot. "They were fine," she said. "Actually, the girls beat all of us up there. I envy them their youthful energy."

"I'm surprised Klaus made it all. He doesn't look as if he's in very good shape."

This wasn't gossip, but pure negativity we were hearing, and I was getting tired of it, too. Agnes looked uncomfortable and asked, "Have you been to Dolly Sods?" to change the subject, I was sure.

"Not in years," I said. "It's a fascinating place. There's no other scenery like it around here, but I'm sure you've read about it."

"We're planning to go tomorrow. Maybe the two of you would like to go with us."

Agnes obviously was trying to dilute the negativity with some positive suggestions. I didn't think I could stand to spend a day in Claudia's company, however. "I'm sorry, but the kids are coming home tonight, so we need to spend some time with them."

Claudia raised her eyebrows. "So they've been located. Took them long enough, didn't it?"

"Just about the right length of time. We were hoping they'd be able to have a decent honeymoon in spite of the terrible situation at the hotel, and they had a week to themselves," Andrea said.

"I understand Stefan is to inherit a fortune from Laszlo," Claudia said.

Andrea stiffened, and I braced myself for what was coming. However, the waitress arrived with a large tray loaded with our plates at that moment, putting off Andrea's answer. When the waitress left, Andrea turned to Claudia. "Laszlo's fortune and Stefan's inheritance aren't subjects we'd discuss, even if we knew anything about them."

At last, Claudia looked as if she'd been put in her place, and I smiled—a trifle maliciously, I admit. "These eggs look wonderful. Let's eat!"

When we finished, Andrea and I decided to have another cup of coffee, and the sisters went on their way, eager to get to Cathedral State Park. I was glad they were gone. "Thanks for putting Claudia in her place. Agnes seems like a nice person. You wonder how she can be related to Claudia."

"Yes, you do wonder. Claudia's a most unpleasant person to be around."

I chuckled. "Almost makes you wish she'd turn out to be the murderer, doesn't it?"

I was surprised when Andrea laughed, too. "It would be good if it turned out that way, but we probably won't have any such luck."

"Good morning. May I join you?"

We looked up at Willard, the one constant in our lives when we were somewhere food was being served. "Of course," I said. Maybe he'd have news for us.

The waitress came and brought him his usual, coffee and two biscuits, without even bothering to take an order. "I suppose you heard that Maggie and Stefan have been found. They should be returning to the hotel by this evening."

"Yes, the sheriff told us last night," Andrea said. "We're most eager to see them."

"I saw the two sisters leaving the lodge as I was coming in. They didn't recognize me, but I knew them. How could I forget that one . . . I think her name's Claudia something. She's a real bear to interview after a crime."

"I think she's a real bear most of the time," I said, knowing Andrea was probably thinking it but wouldn't say it.

She did say, "Have they determined how John Fuller died?"

"Stabbed. In the throat. He was stabbed several times, but the first one probably killed him. No one heard anything, including the Gorsky woman who's in the room across the hall from his. Probably an angry perpetrator is our guess. When you get several stab wounds like that, you know . . ." He took a bite of biscuit.

"Any leads on who might have committed the murders?" I asked.

"None yet. It seems several people had reason to hate Laszlo. The poisoning makes it seem like it was a woman. It's a traditional woman's crime. That, and the fact that there was evidence of sexual activity in Laszlo's case."

Andrea finished her coffee. "Have they finished analyzing the tea bags they found in his room?"

"Nothing there but routine herbs found in herbal tea. Someone managed to add the foxglove to his tea, and then the sexual activity that followed was too much for his heart with the foxglove in his system. Ward told me about the flashlight you found and turned over to him. Good work."

"Thanks," Andrea said. I figured credit for all the detective work had to go to Andrea—I was only an interested bystander—so I didn't say anything. I was just relieved the tea bags didn't contain any foxglove. This revelation surely cleared Maggie and Stefan of any involvement in Laszlo's death.

Willard had wolfed down both biscuits by this time and was finishing his coffee. He set down his cup and wiped his mouth. "Hadley has made a decision about her career. She's changing her major from criminology to hospitality management. I agreed with her that it's a good decision. Lots of tourism here, and if the two of us get serious, which is

98

likely to happen, then both of us working for the sheriff's department might be a problem."

We didn't say anything about Hadley telling us of this change, since she had told us before she told Willard. Andrea simply said, "I imagine finding two bodies was quite a shock to her, and enough to make her think twice about a career in criminology."

We walked out together and went our separate ways. Andrea was in a hurry now to get back to the hotel for a thorough search of Laszlo's room, and we went straight up the stairs when we got there. The yellow tape still remained across the door, but Andrea opened the door and stooped under the tape. I followed, knowing that if Andrea did it, somehow or other we wouldn't be in any trouble.

The first thing Andrea did was to get down on the floor beside the bed Laszlo had been found in. She took out her keychain flashlight and started shining it around and then reached for something by the top leg of the bed.

I had been going through the drawers of the chest, taking out all of Laszlo's clothes and even going through pockets. "What is it?"

"A button." She got up and laid it on the chest. It was a small button, a sort of mottled brown, the kind that sometimes is used on men's sport shirts and women's casual blouses.

"Do you suppose Laszlo tore off someone's blouse in a fit of passion, and the buttons flew all around?"

"No telling, but if there are any more around here, I'm going to find them."

"I'm surprised the sheriff's team didn't find that."

"It was under the bed leg, beside the roller. Very difficult to see. Here, help me move the bed. Who knows what we'll find."

We moved the bed a foot toward the wall, and she looked where the rollers had been sitting on the other side with no luck. Then we pushed it back the other way, but the one button was all that was there. She went to the other bed and got down beside it, and we moved it around, too, but it provided nothing.

"Let's take the drawers out of the chest and put them on the bed. Then we can move the chest out."

We did this and found nothing behind or under the chest except for a few dust bunnies. Just as I knew she would, Andrea said, "I'll go ask Ivy for the vacuum cleaner, and we'll vacuum those up before we put the chest back."

I continued to go through Laszlo's clothes, and Andrea came back with a vacuum cleaner she said she'd retrieved from a linen closet at the end of the upstairs hallway. It took her only a minute to clean up the offending dust bunnies, and we moved the chest back. I had finished going through the clothes, so we put the drawers back, too. Then I started on the few things hanging in the closet.

"I haven't seen anything of Laszlo's suitcase. I guess the sheriff took it," I said.

Andrea had started looking through a small cabinet in the bathroom. "I'm wondering, too, if he had a cell phone. Maybe he left it at home, if he didn't have one that would work here."

"Something tells me he'd have one that would work all over the world, since he was such a big businessman. They do make phones that'll work anywhere, don't they?"

"Yes, and you're right, he probably did have one."

Andrea admitting I might be right about something was a special event, and I felt even more special when I felt something in the inner pocket of a sports jacket. "Eek!" I shrieked and dropped it on the floor.

"It's only a condom, still in its wrapper," she said with her eternal clinical attitude.

"There's something else, too." I pulled out a slip of paper. It was wrinkled and worn-looking, as if it had been carried around for some time. "There's a number on it."

"Hold it by the edge and put it on the chest. It might be possible there are fingerprints." She looked at the number. "It's a local phone number, or part of one. Some digits are missing. It looks like the paper's been in that pocket for a long time."

How she knew it was a local number I don't know. I finished going through the closet and started on the nightstand. I took the drawer out and sorted through the few items there— a pair of sunglasses in a case, a West Virginia map and guidebook, and a granola bar in a worn-looking wrapper. I put the granola bar on the chest, too, just in case.

100

Andrea came back from the bathroom and moved the nightstand away from the wall, vacuumed under it, and put it back. "I'll put the vacuum cleaner away and bring a plastic bag from the kitchen to put this stuff in."

"Maybe we should keep the button to see if it matches the ones on someone's shirt," I said when she came back.

"They're not going to wear that shirt again. The button is probably what they were looking for. They realized they'd lost one and feared it was in this room somewhere. That shirt is hidden away here in the hotel or in some trashcan somewhere in the valley."

She carefully placed the items in the bag and zipped it. "I'll put this in our room till we get a chance to see the sheriff. I don't think there's anything of great urgency here, and he'll probably want to talk to Maggie and Stefan when they get here. I think we should go over to Davis and find a florist and get some flowers for Maggie's and Stefan's rooms. Don't you think that would be a nice gesture?"

"I think it would be very nice. Do you remember seeing a florist there?"

"No, but I asked Ivy when I was downstairs getting the plastic bag, and she said she thinks there is. She couldn't remember what it's called. She's looking it up in the phone book and will tell us when we go downstairs."

The phone book was open on the desk when we went downstairs. "I was confused. There's a Steven's Florist in Parsons, on Poplar Street. That must have been where I saw a florist shop."

"Let's drive over to Parsons—it's not that far," Andrea said. "We'll take the scenic route."

Taking the scenic route with Andrea meant I'd be scared to death. "If Asbury isn't busy, why not have him take over the desk and go with us," I said to Ivy.

"He and David have gone off somewhere to find a part for the faucet he was fixing. It's dripping again. No telling when they'll be back."

"We'd better go on, then," Andrea said.

We went to our room and got our purses. "I guess we should take the things we found with us," Andrea said. "After all, Parsons is the county seat. Ward may be at his office."

I buckled up as soon as we got in the car and clenched my teeth as we whizzed around the curves all the way to Parsons. We found the courthouse first—the huge red structure was easy to spot. We found Ward in his office and explained what we had found, and this time he offered us both a job. On the other hand, he seemed slightly miffed that his men had missed these items.

He walked out to the car with us and pointed us toward the florist shop, where we bought two large bouquets of summery flowers and two inexpensive vases to put them in. Then we rushed back to the Alpenhof, picking up two sandwiches along the way to have for supper.

We put the flowers in water, got the key to Stefan's room from Ivy, and took the flowers upstairs to the rooms. We'd noticed how neat Maggie's room was when we were in there before, and Stefan's was just as neat, with bed made, curtains open to the sun, and books and magazines neatly arranged on their shelves. We put the flowers on the chest in each room, then locked up and went back downstairs.

"I'm hungry, but it occurred to me that everyone might want to go out to eat when the kids get here."

"I'm hungry too. Let's eat the sandwiches, and we can have a garden salad if everybody wants to eat out tonight."

We offered to share with Ivy, but she declined, having had a big meal at lunch. We sat at the fireplace with our sandwiches and drinks from the machine. The hotel was quiet, so quiet I was wondering where everyone was. "Do you suppose they're all out sight-seeing?"

"Either that or taking naps in their rooms."

The whole group drifted in gradually, everyone but Juliet Gorsky, that is, and they all congregated in the lobby to wait for Maggie and Stefan. The men brought chairs from the kitchen, and we all sat around chatting. Even Claudia and Agnes said a few words to Erika. I couldn't help thinking that Claudia must want something from Erika or Franz to bring about this sudden change in attitude.

Andrea's cell phone rang, and she talked for a few minutes. "The kids are in Davis. They stopped to get a burger, but they're on their way now and should be here shortly."

We all cheered in spite of the fact that their honeymoon had been cut short by two ghastly murders.

CHAPTER NINE

Both Maggie and Stefan looked well, in spite of the shock they must have had when the deputy stopped them in Buena Vista. Andrea says it's in Virginia, and it's pronounced not like the Spanish word Buena, but like Buna. Where she gets all her information, I don't know. Probably from the Internet.

We all sat around and questioned them about their trip. They spent three nights at The Greenbrier, and the water pump had given out in Maggie's old Volvo while they were sight-seeing around White Sulphur Springs. They left it in a garage, rented a car, and drove over to the Skyline Drive and headed north. They found interesting old hotels in small towns along the way, and spent time hiking wherever they could find a trail. When they reached the end of the Skyline Drive, they made their way to Harper's Ferry, where they spent two days on the Appalachian Trail, so I wasn't too far off in guessing where they were. They came back to Front Royal and continued south, planning to spend time seeing the rest of the Skyline Drive and part of the Blue Ridge Parkway. The rhododendrons were still blooming, and they had hundreds of photos they'd share with us later.

It was a happy time in spite of the recent grim happenings, and we chatted so long that those who hadn't eaten wouldn't be able to find a restaurant still open. Andrea and I helped Ivy warm up chicken noodle soup and make grilled cheese sandwiches, which everyone seemed to enjoy. Andrea and I shared a grilled cheese. I couldn't help wondering whether Stefan had any idea of the money he'd inherited from Laszlo. Did he know about the will? Maybe he had known of Laszlo's intentions for years, and just hadn't told Maggie. Surely Franz knew and would tell him soon if he didn't know about it. It was comforting to know that Maggie would be well off for the rest of her life.

Since all the family members who had been in the hotel when Laszlo and John died were hanging out in the lobby with Maggie and Stefan, I couldn't resist studying shirts and blouses to see if a button was missing. But I guess what Andrea said earlier was true—whoever had killed Laszlo would never wear that shirt again, so my attempt was futile. I suppose I was hoping someone had run out of clean clothes and in desperation had put on the shirt with the missing button. Then it occurred to me that Juliet wasn't present, and I wondered whether she might own a shirt with a missing button.

Andrea was sitting beside me, and she turned and murmured, "We need to talk to Maggie and Stefan about her computer before they go upstairs. I asked them to join us in our room when everyone's gone."

I had completely forgotten about the sheriff having the computer removed from Maggie's room, and being reminded of it now caused a reversal of my happy mood at seeing the kids. How would they react to the news? They probably would be worried, and I'd make it my business to be as reassuring as possible.

David, Nicole, and Amalie went toward the girls' room, probably to play video games into the night, and the rest of the group began drifting away, too. Erika, Andrea, and I insisted on helping Ivy clean up the kitchen, and Asbury went with Stefan to get the luggage from the car, which they placed by the staircase.

Asbury went out the back door, and everyone else had disappeared from the lobby. The four of us went to our room, where Andrea explained about finding Maggie's computer on, what the deputy found there, and that the computer had been taken away.

I was relieved that their reaction was disbelief and anger rather than worry. "Somebody actually sneaked into my room and used my computer while we were in Parsons checking on our flowers!" Maggie said.

Stefan shook his head. "Why would someone do that? Everyone has a computer these days."

"It's possible they were trying to create suspicion of Maggie, or maybe both of you," Andrea said. "It's lucky you both have a good alibi for that day. That's the day we arrived, and Ivy had told us you were in Parsons."

"But I used the computer after that," Maggie said.

"Yes, and we think they came back. Maybe they were being nosy about your honeymoon plans."

"But how would they get into her room?" Stefan asked, and Andrea explained about the hotel keys.

I had planned to be reassuring, but I hadn't said a word. Maybe this would help: "Andrea and I both told Ward that you were at the florist's that day. That and the fact that the computer was wiped clean of fingerprints should take away any suspicion of the two of you."

They left, not showing any signs of worry, but doing something positive—they were already making plans to beef up security in the hotel as they walked out. After a few minutes, Maggie called Andrea's cell phone to thank us for the flowers. I hoped they would brighten things up after what must have been a real downer on their return.

"I think they took that pretty well," I said.

"I do, too. We had to do it before they went upstairs tonight. She might have gone into her room, and explaining what happened after she discovered her computer was gone would have been worse."

I went to the window and looked out, but the picnic table was vacant. "Did you notice how friendly Claudia was to Erika and Franz? I couldn't help thinking she must want something from them."

Of course Andrea had noticed. She notices everything. "Yes, I did, and thought it was quite a turnaround from the scene we saw at the Blackwater Lodge the other day."

"I looked over all the shirts. No one had a button missing."

Andrea laughed. "No one's going to wear that shirt. Maybe we should look in the dumpster."

"Where's the dumpster?"

"It's on the other side of the hotel from our room. There's a gravel road that leads off the parking lot and goes back there."

"I never noticed. I don't suppose it would be too sanitary, looking in there. Besides, the deputies probably checked it already."

"They checked Laszlo's room, too, but look what we found. I noticed when I got the vacuum cleaner from upstairs that there's a box of vinyl gloves in that closet. I could use those. Of course, it's possible the dumpster's been emptied since the murders."

"Have you thought about the fact that while David and Nicole are mooning around outside our window, Amalie can come and go as she wishes without anyone knowing she's even been out of the room."

"I've thought about a lot of things without having proof of anything. Someone here's a killer—possibly two someones if Laszlo and John were murdered by different people. There's just no proof to show us who it is."

Two killers running loose in the hotel—the idea was doubly chilling. I headed for a hot shower as Andrea braced the door with the chair and locked it.

#

We had breakfast before starting the dumpster project. We didn't see anyone we knew at the lodge, so we ate quickly and got back to the hotel as soon as we could. I went upstairs and got the whole box of vinyl gloves from the linen closet—who knew how many it might take. Andrea explained to Asbury what she planned to do, and told him she wanted a ladder to help her get into the dumpster. He brought a small folding ladder, just the right size, and set it up alongside the dumpster.

I had planned on getting in there with Andrea, but she said she would do it alone. I was to hold plastic bags from the kitchen and seal up anything she found that might be of interest. However, when Asbury insisted on helping her, she agreed. Both wearing vinyl gloves, they started going through loose stuff. Since the hotel doesn't have a restaurant, there was no organic material to be dealt with.

After each loose piece of trash was thoroughly looked over, they put it in one of the trash bags Asbury had brought. He quite often asked Andrea to look at something; we've often wondered just how well Asbury can read. One of them found a poem written on a sheet of lined paper. They dropped it into one of my bags, and I read it through the plastic:

Disappointment
You weren't there for me

My life was ready to open
Into a luscious blossom of red
But you weren't there
So I felt you ebbing away
Leaving me as you always do
But this time it's forever.

It sounded like a murderer's poem to me. The handwriting was small and cramped, and when I turned it over, words in a foreign language were written on the back. My guess was German, and what was written there was in seven lines, with a single word at the top. It undoubtedly was the same poem, written first in German and then translated into English. "Very interesting," I said into the dumpster.

Andrea simply grunted as she tugged a large trash bag free of some others and started opening it. They had finished with the loose trash and were looking into the bags.

Asbury held up a cell phone.

I opened a plastic bag. "That's great, Asbury! I wonder if it's Laszlo's."

"I hope the memory card's in it," Andrea said.

I had no idea what a memory card is. I have a cell phone for emergencies, but all I know is to punch 911 or Andrea's number. "I guess the deputies haven't gone through this trash. They surely would have found the cell phone." I set the bags with the poem and phone on a rock next to the dumpster.

It took them the rest of the morning to finish. They had dropped each completed bag over the side, so the dumpster was bare. At least, it looked bare to me. That's when Andrea spotted something small and black in a corner. It appeared to have been stuck in some goo when she reached down and picked it up.

"It's a memory card...but it's a mess." She dropped it into my waiting plastic bag, and it stuck to the side on the way to the bottom.

I lifted the ladder over the rim to them, and they climbed up and slid down the side of the dumpster. All three of us began throwing the trash bags back in. Andrea and Asbury took off their gloves and tossed those, too.

"Let's go to the room and put this stuff away till we can get it to the sheriff." Andrea said. "I want to take a shower and wash these clothes."

"Hand your clothes out to me, and I'll start them in the laundry while you shower," I said when she had gone into the bathroom.

When I got to the laundry room, Karla was there again. This time she had both washers going. "I'll be through soon," she said.

"I'm not in a hurry." *This must be the cleanest family in Germany*, I thought. How to make conversation? "I understand your husband is a pharmacist."

"Yes. He has a drug store."

"How do drug stores in Germany compare to those here?"

"About the same. Ours is small, and the ones we went to here are small too."

Aha! So they've been going to drug stores here. Interesting. What else to talk about? "Are the girls enjoying their visit to the Canaan Valley?"

"They like it very much here, but they are ready to go home now. Amalie is, anyway. Nicole is friends with David, so she enjoys that. They will email each other when we go home."

I couldn't help wondering whether David had a computer. I hadn't seen one at the house, but it's undoubtedly in his room. Otherwise, maybe he borrows Stefan's or Maggie's. It was possible that Asbury and Ivy couldn't afford an Internet connection.

Just then Maggie came in carrying a laundry bag. "I didn't know anyone was in here. What were you and Andrea doing at the dumpster?"

"Where were you? We didn't see you."

"I was upstairs, and I walked down the hallway to the end of the building to look out that window in the hallway at my flower garden. I was wondering if it got enough water while I was gone. There was Andrea and someone else, maybe Asbury, inside the dumpster. What on earth were they doing?"

I hesitated for a moment, not wanting to discuss our playing detective in front of Karla. "Andrea lost her address book, and she thought maybe it would be in the trash. She found it, and she's getting a shower. I'm getting ready to wash her clothes. Did you say flower garden? I didn't notice a flower garden."

"It's on beyond the dumpster. We're getting ready to clear off that empty lot and make something of it, so I started a flower garden at the edge of it last year. Come on out, both of you, and I'll show you."

Karla shook her head. "My clothes are about ready to go into the dryers. I'll go look later."

Maggie and I started through the lobby just as Andrea came out of the hallway. "We're going out to see my flower garden. Come with us."

"I didn't know you had a flower garden," Andrea said. "Where is it?"

"It's on the lot adjacent to the hotel. Stefan owns that, too. We're going to put something there, but we're not sure what."

"A nice lawn for croquet would be good," I said. "I used to love playing croquet."

Maggie laughed and then began to look as if she were considering my suggestion. "Maybe you have something there. We could have flowers all around and a croquet area in the center. Maybe we can revive croquet as a national sport."

We followed her out the front door and around to the side of the building. On past the dumpster I could see a weedy area with several trees, but on one side of this area was a small flower bed. Everything was blooming profusely, and bees were buzzing all around. "I just bought a few packets of seeds, and all this came up," Maggie said. "We've had quite a bit of rain since I planted the seeds, and that's helped."

"What are all these flowers?" Andrea asked. She's not much of a gardener.

"These at the edge are impatiens. I don't remember all the names, to tell you the truth. I think that one's a lady slipper, and that's some kind of daisy. Those at the back are foxglove. I planted all the seeds last year, but the foxglove didn't bloom until this year."

Foxglove. Where had I heard that word? Oh, foxglove! The plant that was used to poison Laszlo. I looked at Andrea, and she was looking at Maggie. "Did you know it was digitalis, which is derived from foxglove, that was used to poison Laszlo?"

"No! My God! I wonder . . ."

She didn't have to finish that sentence. She was wondering, just as Andrea and I were, whether the foxglove that was used came from the flower garden. They were such beautiful, bell-shaped flowers in pink and yellow. Who would have thought the plant could be fatal?

"This will be the last year for foxglove in the garden," she said. "Stefan's going to be so upset if we find out it was the foxglove I planted that poisoned Laszlo."

"Neither of you had any way of knowing that something like this could happen. Knowing that this is growing here makes this seem like possibly a spur-of-the-moment crime rather than something premeditated. Of course, whoever killed him could have brought it with them, too."

"Let's go back to the hotel," I said. "I wasn't able to start your laundry because Karla was using both washers."

Karla had put her things in the dryers when we got back, so I tossed Andrea's clothes into one washer and Maggie used the other. "What's Stefan doing today?" I asked.

"He and David are putting up two-by-fours in the attic. They're framing another room. One of these days we may have enough for everyone who wants to stay here during the ski season."

"I thought I heard pounding earlier, but it was faint."

"They've insulated the floor up there real well so the upstairs guests won't disturb the ones on the second floor."

"Do you plan to install an elevator to take people up there?"

"Not really. There are lots of hotels in Europe with no elevators. Stefan likes that idea, and I do, too. The guests who stay in the attic rooms will be skiers or hikers, so it won't be a problem."

Andrea had gone ahead to our room, and Maggie and I decided to join her while the clothes were washing. We sat on the beds, and Andrea said, "We need to find out who was staying in the four rooms on the end of the hotel that faces the flower garden before, during, and after the wedding."

"There was no one in any of those rooms up until the day of the wedding, and there's been no one since that I know of. It was just that one night."

"John Fuller was in one of the end rooms downstairs after Laszlo died, but of course he wasn't here on the weekend of the wedding," I said.

"Let's look at the register and get the names. I'm just wondering if anyone saw something from the windows on that end. These are all friends of Stefan's and yours, aren't they?"

"Yes, they are. Let's go to the lobby."

"I think Ivy deserves an explanation of what's going on, don't you?" I said.

"Yes, I'll tell her what's happening while Maggie gets the names."

We went to the lobby, and Andrea started explaining. "We discovered Maggie has foxglove growing in her flower garden, and it was this plant or the drug derived from it that killed Laszlo. Maggie's checking to see who stayed in the rooms on that side of the hotel so we can check to see if they saw anything."

Maggie jotted down names on a pad from behind the desk. "Four friends of ours were in the downstairs rooms, two to a room. One of our ski school buddies was in one of the end rooms upstairs, and in the other room, a couple who also work at the school. I've been meaning to call her—she has a new baby, a girl who was born shortly before the wedding. Anyway, I have all these people in my phone book, and I'll call and ask if they saw anything the night they were here." She went to the couch with her list and started pushing buttons on her cell phone.

Andrea and I sat on the chairs across the coffee table from her, hoping to hear something that would help clear up the mystery of who killed Laszlo. The first three attempts brought nothing but an answering machine, and she left messages, asking them to call her. On the fourth call, she obviously was talking to a person and not a machine. "Hi, Suzy! No, we're back at the hotel now. Some problems developed here while we were gone, and we had to come back early.

"Two people died, and the sheriff's saying both were murdered. I know, we can't believe it either. One of them was Stefan's Uncle Laszlo. We're not sure. No, the other was a man who was involved with Laszlo in various business ventures. Anyway, I wanted to ask . . . no, they don't know yet who killed them. But I wanted to ask you, when you were here on the night of the wedding, you were in one of the end rooms. Did you happen to see anything from your windows on that end of the hotel? From the time you checked in till you left.

"No, well, it's just that the sheriff wanted me to ask. I'm not sure why. Anyway, it was great seeing you. Thanks so much for coming, and thanks for the gift. I'll be writing you. Yes. Goodbye."

Maggie laid the phone on the coffee table. "I didn't want to lie to her, but I thought maybe I shouldn't tell her why we want to know at this point. I just added the part about the sheriff and not knowing why so I wouldn't have to explain."

Her phone rang again, and she went through a similar conversation with someone named Jennifer. When she was through, she said, "I'll try the ones who stayed upstairs," and again she left messages to be called back.

"What did we do before answering machines—or whatever it is that takes a message on a cell phone," I said. Then it occurred to me that I hadn't told Maggie what Andrea and Asbury were really looking for in the dumpster. "I said Andrea lost her address book, but that was a lie, too. I just didn't want to say what they were looking for in front of Karla. They were looking for clues to the murders."

"Did they find anything?"

"There was an interesting hand-written poem in there, all crumpled up, but the main thing was a cell phone. Then in the bottom of the bin was a memory card. It's all in plastic bags, waiting for the sheriff to come by and get it. He said he'll be over sometime this evening."

"I was hoping we could all go out to eat this evening. Maybe he'll come before we leave," Maggie said.

"If not, I'll stay here and wait for him. You can bring me a sandwich," Andrea said.

Maggie's phone rang again, and she went through the conversation a third time. However, this time the person on the other end of the line seemed to have heard of the murders. "That was Charlie Evans. He and his wife were in the upstairs room on the right side of the hallway. He's at work. He's working in maintenance at the lodge till ski season begins again. He said Isabelle, his wife, is home with the baby. She doesn't have a phone. How would you like to drive over to her place? I sent them a gift for the baby, but I need to pay a visit to see her."

"That would be a good idea," Andrea said. "Shall we take my car?"

"Let's take the Volvo. I know the way."

I was hoping it wouldn't break down on us as we got in and started for Cortland Road, where Charlie and Isabelle lived. Their house was tiny but neat-looking, with an old-fashioned porch on the front. Maggie knocked on the screen door, and we heard someone walking inside. Isabelle turned out to be a tall, thin woman with dark hair pulled back and fastened with a rubber band. She and Maggie hugged, and she asked us in.

After the introductions were over, Isabelle said, "We've heard about the murders at the hotel. I understand one of the men who were killed was Stefan's uncle."

"Yes," Maggie said, "it was his Uncle Laszlo Novacek from the Czech Republic. Stefan was totally devastated by the news. He's insisting we go ahead with the work we've been doing on the attic, and I think he's finding the carpentry therapeutic after the shock of Laszlo's death."

"Have they found out who did it?"

"No, but they're definitely working on it. But we came to see the baby, and then I have a question for you."

"Cara's asleep right now. Come in the nursery and you can see her."

We followed her into a small bedroom with a bassinette on one side. Cara looked angelic as she snoozed away. "She's darling," Maggie said, and Andrea and I agreed. I was struck by the contrast between our errand, one more attempt to find out who committed two gruesome murders, and the sweet innocence of the beautiful sleeping child.

Isabelle led us back to the living room, where the three of us squeezed onto the couch, leaving the only chair in the room for her. She went to the kitchen for iced tea, and when she returned, she brought not only the tea but a plateful of store-bought gingersnaps.

Maggie sipped her tea. "When you were in the upstairs room on the night of the wedding, did you happen to look out the window?"

"Yes, I went to the window because I wondered what was on that side of the hotel."

"Did you see anything unusual?"

"Not really. Well, there was something . . . we had finished eating after the ceremony and went back upstairs to use the bathroom. It was getting dark when I looked out the window. There was someone out there. I didn't realize you had a flower garden on that side of the hotel, or at least it looked like a flower garden in the fading light."

"I started that last year. We're planning to do something with that lot, but we're not sure what. But was the person you saw looking at the flower garden?"

"It looked like she was picking flowers. I only looked out for a minute, and then Charlie was ready to go back downstairs. I thought possibly it was Ivy, but I couldn't think why she'd be picking flowers, when there were so many for the wedding."

"It definitely was a woman, then?"

"Yes, she had on a dress. It was dark enough that I couldn't really tell what color it was. It was a light color, though, which is probably the reason I noticed her."

All the women at the wedding had been wearing light-colored summer dresses, so that didn't help much. At least we knew it was a woman. "Any concept of her age?" I asked.

"I couldn't tell. There wasn't enough light. What's the significance of someone being out there at the flower garden?"

Maggie obviously had found it easier to lie on the phone than in person, so she explained the situation with the foxglove and asked Isabelle to tell no one but Charlie, and to ask Charlie not to say anything.

I hoped that would happen, but knowing how news spreads in small communities, I had my doubts. Maybe the murders would be solved before rumors could spread. We helped ourselves to a couple of gingersnaps and finished our tea. I couldn't think of anything more to ask, and I guess the others couldn't either, so we took a last look at peacefully sleeping Cara, thanked Isabelle, and said goodbye.

The Volvo was humming right along as we rode home. Maggie's so attached to it because she inherited it from her father, and I don't suppose she'll ever let it go. I keep hoping it'll continue running well for her.

"I've been meaning to ask you something, Maggie," I said. "Do you have any idea who Juliet Gorsky is and why she showed up at the hotel?"

"I have no idea. I never heard of her before. We told Laszlo to bring a friend if he wanted to, but he never said anything about her. She just showed up."

I thought about this for a while. "Something else I've been wondering about. Isabelle and her husband live so close, why did they stay at the hotel that night?" I asked.

"They probably thought we'd be serving something alcoholic and didn't want to drive if they'd been drinking. Of course we served nothing but iced tea and soft drinks, but they didn't know what the plan was."

That's our Maggie, I thought. *Frugal to the core.*

#

Stefan was in the lobby when we got back, looking good in jeans and a button-down shirt. He hugged all of us. "Are we going out to eat tonight? I'm starving."

"I'll see if I can round up the others."

"I'm going to stay here," Andrea said. "I'm supposed to meet the sheriff, and I don't know what time he'll be here."

Stefan looked as if he wondered why Andrea was meeting the sheriff, but only said, "Tell him to meet us at the lodge. He can eat with us."

"I'll see if I can reach him." She started for our room.

"I'm thinking we should ask Juliet if she wants to go with us. We haven't seen much of her since the wedding," I said.

Stefan started down the hallway. "I'll check her room." When he got back, "She didn't answer the door. She must be out somewhere."

Gradually the whole group straggled into the lobby, and Andrea came back, too. "I'll go with you. Ward said he'd meet us there." She was carrying her large purse, and I knew she had the evidence stowed in there. Again, I was thinking there were thirteen of us. At least the sheriff would make fourteen. I just hoped he'd get there quickly before any bad luck could befall us.

Eva Weiss walked up just as we were going out the door. She threw her arms around Stefan's neck. "I heard you were back! Why didn't you let me know?"

He untangled himself and stepped back. "We just got back last night, and we've been busy getting caught up."

Erika came over to them. "We're going to the lodge for dinner. Why don't you join us?"

"I'd love to, but I don't have my purse. I'll run back to the house . . ."

"Don't worry about it," Franz said. Obviously he was planning to pay again.

She turned and started to her house. "My lipstick! I need my lipstick! Pick me up over there."

"Let's ride with someone else, because Ward wants to give me a ride back here," Andrea said to me, so we went with Maggie and Stefan, riding in the Volvo once again.

Tables were moved together at the restaurant to make room for such a large group. Nicole must have invited David, because the two of them were sitting together across from us. My worry about a group of thirteen was wasted tonight. Amalie was beside me, and again I was challenged with making conversation with someone who might not understand all my comments.

After we'd all ordered, I said to her, "Are you enjoying your stay in the valley?"

"Yes, very much. But now I'm ready to go home. I'm working this summer for my father, earning money for school in the fall."

She and Nicole started speaking to each other in German, and I was relieved for the moment of trying to think what to say next. The other sisters were at the end of the table. Claudia was next to Franz, and Agnes was beside Klaus Becker. I couldn't help noticing that Stefan sat down quickly beside his mother and held Maggie's hand as she sat down on the other side. He obviously wasn't taking any chances with Eva sitting next to him. She was left to sit beside Claudia, and they immediately began chatting in German. Ward hadn't shown up yet, but there was room for an additional chair at the table when he did. No one had considered waiting for him to order, so I hoped he'd come soon.

117

The waitress was bringing our drinks when he walked in. It would have been convenient if he'd be able to sit beside Andrea, but it would have been awkward if I'd moved to the chair that was being brought up, so he sat beside Maggie. He gave her a hug, and she introduced him to the others at the table. He'd questioned some of them after the murders, but no one mentioned this and it was obvious it hadn't occurred to Maggie.

The meal went off quietly, with no drama and no fireworks. When the bill came, Franz and Stefan argued over who would pay. Andrea and I insisted on leaving the tip, but Stefan said it was included in the bill, with such a large group. He finally won out and gave the waitress his credit card. I noticed she'd given Ward a separate bill. He didn't want to be obligated to anyone in our group, it seemed, not even for a meal, and I figured he'd asked the waitress for a separate bill before coming to the table.

"We're opening wedding presents tomorrow," Maggie announced to the group before we left the table. "Come to the lobby at four."

What with two murders, we'd all forgotten about the wedding presents, so a pleasant murmur spread around the table. This would be a nice diversion from fearful thoughts of a murderer running loose in the hotel.

When we all went out to the parking lot, Andrea got some curious looks when she got into Ward's car and they drove away. Erika walked over to my side. "Do I detect a budding romance there?"

I just smiled and shrugged my shoulders, hoping it was so. The two of them still hadn't returned to the hotel when I got back with Maggie and Stefan. We all said goodnight in the lobby and went to our rooms. I had a shower and was reading in bed when I heard muffled noises from the room above, which was Stefan's. His room was the largest in the hotel, encompassing the back side of the east wing. It took up as much space as the two rooms opposite it on that wing. I supposed Maggie had moved in there with him, and that eventually her room would be turned into another guest room.

Finally Andrea came in. I wanted to ask what had taken her so long, but she gets irritated with my nosiness, so I didn't say anything. She volunteered this: "I explained to Ward about the flower garden with the foxglove growing in it, and told him about our conversation with Isabelle, how she'd seen a woman out there on the night of Laszlo's death. And, of course, I gave him the things we found in the dumpster."

"He must have been pleased with all this information."

"He was."

"I suppose he wasn't pleased that the deputies missed the items from the dumpster."

"He wasn't."

Just then we heard more noises from upstairs. "I suppose that's Maggie and Stefan in his room," I said.

She grabbed her flashlight. "It could be the linen closet up there. I'm going to the laundry room to see if anyone comes down the attic stairs."

A chill ran up my spine, but I got up and put on my robe to follow her.

CHAPTER TEN

Ivy was no longer at the desk, and the only light was a dim one over her station. I decided to sit down on the couch, where I could watch the kitchen and the door to the laundry room, which Andrea had left open, and also the main stairway, in case someone came down there. There was no sound whatsoever, and I wasn't happy being alone here in the semi-darkness, but I figured the best thing I could do would be to keep a lookout on both areas.

I sat there for what seemed like ten minutes and didn't hear anything. Surely if someone were upstairs and needed to come down, they would have done it by now. The only people who were supposed to be on the second floor were Maggie and Stefan. There were no guests up there. I decided to walk into the laundry room and see what Andrea was doing, and when I got there, the door to the attic stairs was open, but Andrea was nowhere in sight. She must have gone up the stairs, but I didn't have my flashlight, and I wasn't about to walk up those spooky stairs at night, even if I did have it. She must have gone up to check out the linen closet on the second floor.

I sneaked over to the main stairway and climbed as quietly as I could. I could see that there was a faint light burning in the hallway of the second floor. When I got to the top, I noticed that the door to the linen closet was open, and Andrea's legs were sticking back into the hallway. "What are you doing?" I whispered over her shoulder.

She jumped. "You almost gave me a heart attack! The bottom shelf of this closet's a mess. I have a feeling someone hid something here and they were retrieving it tonight. I wish I had searched it when I was looking in here before."

We heard a car pull into the parking lot, then a car door shut. We hurried down the hallway and heard the front door of the hotel open. Someone was slipping down one of the hallways, and we couldn't be sure which one it was. When we got to the top of the stairs, all was quiet below. The door to the hotel was standing slightly ajar.

"They must have come down the main stairs while I was still getting my robe on, because I came out and watched the stairs for about ten minutes," I said. "Maybe they went out, leaving the front door unlocked so they could get back in."

"Or maybe it was Nicole coming back from somewhere in their rental car."

"I guess she could have gotten back in if she left the door unlocked when she left."

"What are you two doing out here?" This time we both jumped. It was Stefan, standing behind us in his pajama bottoms.

"We heard noises up here above our room and came up to investigate," Andrea said.

"It was probably Maggie and me getting ready for bed."

"I don't think so." Andrea explained the sequence of events to him, including those we were surmising.

Then he saw that the door was ajar. "With a murderer running around, we can't have that." He went downstairs, shut the door, and turned the deadbolt.

I didn't point out to him that the murderer was undoubtedly inside the hotel right now and couldn't be locked out. Now Maggie came out, tying her robe. "What's going on?"

Stefan was climbing the stairs. "Back to bed, everybody. I'll explain to you in the room." He put his arm around her and ushered her through the door.

"Goodnight," we both whispered, and headed for our room.

"Stefan has quite a physique, hasn't he?" I asked when we got there.

"He's a healthy-looking specimen, all right. He and Maggie both are. I suppose it's all the skiing and hiking."

"Do you think they know about the inheritance?"

"I've no idea. Maggie hasn't said anything."

"It sounds like they'll be set for life. I just hope they won't sell the hotel and go off to live in Europe."

"Something tells me they're happy here and enjoy running the hotel, no matter how much money they have. They love the ski school and being in the Ski Patrol."

"I wonder if they have the Ski Patrol in Europe."

"I have no idea."

Something Andrea didn't know. That always makes me feel good. But then she'll probably be researching it on the Internet at the first opportunity. I got into bed. "Speaking of money, it would be interesting to find out who else was involved in the venture where Klaus lost all his money. If John Fuller was a partner with Laszlo in that, it would prove the same person killed them both."

"I can't think of any reason someone would kill both of them unless it had to do with money. Of course, we don't know all the facts yet. Maybe someone had an affair with both of them that ended badly, and decided to get even while in the mountains of West Virginia. I think there's a mistaken idea that small-town sheriffs are easy to fool, but we both know that's not the case with Ward. However, I'm going to talk to Stefan in the morning, and then I'll get on the Internet and see what I can find."

#

"Let's try something different for breakfast," Andrea said as we were getting dressed.

"What would you suggest?"

"There's a bed and breakfast in Davis with a restaurant that's open to the public. It's called the Bright Morning Inn. That might be a nice change."

"When are you going to talk to Stefan?"

"When we get back. They may not even be up yet."

We left for Davis wearing sweaters. The sun was coming up, but there was still a chill in the air. "I don't suppose we're likely to see Willard at a bed and breakfast, so we can't learn the latest. We haven't heard anything about any of the stuff we've been turning over to the sheriff."

"Ward told me last night he talked to Klaus, and he said Laszlo had volunteered to help them with the cost of the trip. That explained the payment to Klaus in Laszlo's checkbook; at least that's the way Klaus explained it."

I thought this over for a minute. "I suppose if Laszlo felt guilty enough about the fact that Klaus lost his money, then that would seem plausible."

After discussing the Beckers on the way to Davis, we were surprised to find them in the Bright Morning Restaurant. I had imagined them being so poor that they were living on peanut butter and crackers in their rooms except for when they were taken out to dinner by Franz. Maybe this was a big splurge for them.

As usual, it was Nicole who caught the eye as soon as we walked in. It wasn't the way she dressed—both girls were wearing jeans and sweatshirts. It was her personality. She came across as temperamental, tempestuous, and ready to try new adventures. Amalie, on the other hand, was quiet and introverted. I would be kind and not think mousey. I couldn't help wondering, not for the first time, whether a new adventure for Nicole might be murdering two people, or talking David into helping her do it.

They were already seated at a table for four, so we greeted them and sat down at a small table for two across from them. We could chat from there, if we could think of anything to say to them. We ordered coffee and looked at the menus. "I'm going to have oatmeal with walnuts and raisins," Andrea said.

"That sounds very healthful." I couldn't bring myself to be quite so healthy, though, and decided on scrambled eggs.

The waitress came back with our coffee, and I added half and half. "Have you folks been to Blackwater Falls?"

Klaus spoke up. It was obvious he spoke the best English of the group, and would always do the talking when he was present. "We're going over there after breakfast. I understand it's a beautiful place."

"You should go in the lodge, too. It's wonderful, and you can always have a mid-morning coffee in the restaurant."

"You can get a map of the park in the lodge, too," Andrea said. "There are some nice hiking trails, with exceptional photo opportunities. Of course, the best opportunity is at the falls."

"We plan to take all that in. Stefan gave me a map."

Food began arriving for both tables, and we got involved in eating. They finished before we did and went on their way, while we lingered over more coffee. "They seem ordinary enough," I said. "It would be difficult to see one of them as a murderer, except for maybe Nicole."

"I think she's just high-spirited, and she seems quite intelligent. Both the girls do, for that matter."

"I don't know how you can tell with Amalie. She never says or does anything."

"She's just quiet. Shy, probably."

Andrea's always an inspiration to me. She never has anything bad to say about anyone, and when something bad is revealed, I can see that it disturbs her in spite of her placid façade. I found myself hoping that neither of the girls was involved in the murders, for Stefan's sake if nothing else.

We drove slowly back to the hotel; Andrea seemed to feel like taking in the scenery for a change. When we got there, we could hear noises coming from upstairs. "Is Stefan working in the attic?" Andrea asked Ivy.

"I think they're all up there, putting up Sheetrock. They're partitioning off another room."

We went to the stairs off the laundry room. This was the only way to get to the attic at present. I imagined that when we came back to the lodge again, the kids would have extended the main staircase to reach what would by then be considered the third floor. Maggie and Stefan were the only ones in the attic. "I sent Asbury and David for more Sheetrock," Stefan said.

Andrea sat down on a sawhorse. "We wanted to do some research online, and thought maybe you could help us. We know that Klaus and Karla lost a lot of money in some sort of business deal with Laszlo. Do you know whether John Fuller was involved in this also?"

"I told Maggie to email you with as much information about my family as we thought would be helpful. That way, in case there were tensions, you could understand. John Fuller had to be involved in that venture, because both his name and Laszlo's were on it somehow. I can't remember the exact name of the business. I understand what you're thinking, that since they both were killed, this puts a lot of suspicion on the Beckers."

"We're only thinking it's a possibility," Andrea said.

"I'd hate to think anyone in my family could commit murder. I'd hate to think Claudia or Agnes could, also. But what reason could anyone else have?"

I moved to sit down beside Andrea, and she scooted over to make room for me. "Did the sisters ever invest in Laszlo's enterprises?" I couldn't bear to ask about Franz and Erika, as if I were suspicious of them.

"I think most everyone in the family did at one time or another. Most of them made money, too, as Laszlo did. It's just that the Beckers happened to invest in what was probably the most disastrous of all Laszlo's ventures, and they didn't have the funds to invest further and recoup their losses.

"I'm feeling really bad about this, since I'm inheriting the bulk of Laszlo's estate. I want to help my cousins with their college educations. Their funds were invested and lost, too. I explained to them yesterday that I'd finance whatever schooling they choose, and after they're through, they're on their own. They're both bright and ambitious, and they'll do okay. Amalie wants to transfer to Heidelberg this fall if she can be admitted."

So, at last we knew that Stefan knew, and of course Maggie knew, too. I thought they'd have been turning cartwheels, but I suppose the murders have put quite a damper on things. Then, too, there's a lot more to the two of them than a desire to have money.

Andrea asked Stefan if she could use his computer, since Maggie's still hadn't been returned, and he gave her his room key. We went to his room, where I would sit on the sidelines and be bored, unless she found something really juicy.

After what seemed like an hour of sitting around, listening to Andrea clicking away at the keyboard, I excused myself and went to our room and got my Ben Rehder novel. I'd spend the rest of the afternoon in the lobby, concentrating on a fictitious and hilarious murder mystery. I hadn't read for long, though, when Ivy suggested we have coffee and cookies. She made a pot earlier. I went to the kitchen and brought two cups of coffee and tin of shortbread cookies, and she joined me in front of the fireplace.

"I wonder if the sheriff's made any progress in figuring out who murdered our guests," she said.

I helped myself to a cookie. "We haven't heard anything. I suppose Asbury told you about the things they found in the dumpster. We haven't had a report on whether they were helpful, but if that phone was Laszlo's, I'd think it would show something. If the memory card can be cleaned up enough to be used, that is."

"What's a memory card?"

It was comforting to know there's someone else who's just as ignorant as I am. What Ivy and I do know a lot about are the signs of the moon. I learned on our last trip to the valley that Ivy is even more knowledgeable about moon signs than I am. Because we have that in common, I feel this kinship with Ivy, and I didn't want to act like I knew a lot about memory cards when I didn't. "It's some kind of little plastic thing that goes inside a phone. Andrea only explained it to me yesterday. I guess the phone information is stored there. It might show who Laszlo's been calling and who's been calling him."

Ivy nodded. "I think it'll be a relief to all of us when they find the murderer. I suppose one person killed them both, and I can't help thinking it has to be someone who's staying in the hotel right now. None of the locals had a reason to murder either of them, and neither did any of Maggie and Stefan's friends who came to the wedding."

"I think you're right. It's going to be interesting this weekend, with the dark of the moon coming up. I can't help wondering what that will bring."

"Not another murder, I hope. Nothing good can happen in the dark of the moon."

I heard Andrea shutting and locking Stefan's door, and she came downstairs, poured herself a cup of coffee, and joined us. I didn't know whether she wanted to talk about what she found in front of Ivy, so I didn't say anything. However, she did. She began by telling Ivy, "We knew some of the relatives had lost money when they invested in a business that Laszlo was part of. I was checking on the Internet to see if anyone else had lost their investment. I found out that everyone here lost some money in the same venture when the Beckers lost everything. I don't know how much, but even the sisters had invested something."

"I wish we knew how much was involved," I said. "The amount could be a clue to the murders."

"I know. Losing a few hundred would be different than losing everything you own."

Ivy got up and returned with the coffeepot. "It sounds to me like any one of the guests could have murdered them. I heard Mr. Fuller was Mr. Novacek's partner. I suppose he was involved in that deal where people lost money, too."

Andrea held out her cup. "Yes, he was. He and Laszlo were partners in that particular venture. It seems the entire family has remained close and stayed in touch through email and instant messaging, so it was only natural they'd be investing with Laszlo."

Oh, dear. Here was something else I didn't know about, but I wasn't going to ask about instant messaging now. "Did you say the sisters lost something? It doesn't seem likely they'd invest with Laszlo."

"They must have been close to the family all along, too, and probably invested through John Fuller."

We were interrupted when the front door opened. Willard walked in wearing his deputy uniform. "I just stopped by to see Hadley. Is she still here?"

"She's cleaning down the hall there." Ivy motioned to the wing where the Beckers were staying.

"Just a minute, Willard," Andrea said. "Sit down with us a minute."

He sat down on the couch beside her.

"What do you hear about all the evidence we've been giving Ward?"

He looked at Ivy, obviously wondering how much he should say.

"Ivy knows about what we found."

"We haven't found any fingerprints on anything. The main thing now is the phone, and there were no fingerprints on that, either. Our tech guy is working on getting the memory card cleaned up without damaging the card, which has been no easy task. Something was stuck all over it, and he thinks it might have been glue."

"Someone was determined to keep the authorities from finding out what was on that card," I said.

"It looks that way. We've been checking all the stores in the area, and no one remembers anyone buying glue since the guests arrived."

"Would you like some coffee?" Ivy asked.

"I'd love it. It's time for a break. I'll go say hi to Hadley first." He got up and went down the hallway, and I went to the kitchen for a cup.

Willard came back and took the coffee I poured for him, and then scooped up a half dozen cookies. Andrea had been looking thoughtful during the conversation about the phone and phone card and not saying much. Something told me an idea was building in her mind, but she wasn't ready to discuss it. It would be no use prodding her; I knew that much for sure. I speak from experience.

Finally she did speak up. "Let's not eat too many cookies. Maggie and Stefan want to take us out to eat tonight."

"Where are you going?" Willard asked.

"Muttley's, in Davis, I think they said."

"You'll like it. Have a steak. They have great steak."

Of course Willard would like any place where food was being served. How he stayed so skinny I'll never know. "Did you see Hadley back there?"

"She's cleaning the girls' room. What a mess that is— clothes and all kinds of junk piled everywhere."

"They're typical teenagers, I guess," I said. "I must say, David has enjoyed having them here. They play video games, and they went to a movie one night. We see David and Nicole sitting on the picnic bench at night, chatting away like teens do."

"I suppose it's harmless enough," Ivy said. "It's just that they're older than he is, but the three of them don't have anyone else around here to socialize with. Jeremy is David's best friend, but he lives somewhere over on the other side of Davis."

Willard picked up a couple more cookies. "I hate to leave good company, but I have to go. Duty calls, you know."

"Can you come back at four?" I asked. "Maggie and Stefan are planning to open wedding presents then."

"I'll try, if there's nothing pressing going on," he said as he went out the door.

I've never been sure just how much attention Willard pays to duty, but I suppose Ward would fire him if he didn't do the job. "What time do Maggie and Stefan want to go?" I asked Andrea.

"They said six. They want to open the presents and get those stored in Maggie's room before we go."

I got up and started gathering up empty cups and the cookie tin. "I'm going to have a shower and take a nap."

Andrea followed me to the kitchen. "Me, too. I'll help you with the cups."

Ivy yelled after us, "Don't worry about those things. I'll get them. There's no one checking in today."

"Relax, Ivy," I said. "We'll do it."

#

We both lay down after our showers and promptly went to sleep. It seemed like no time at all until someone was knocking on our door. We were already in jeans and sweaters, makeup on, and all we had to do was straighten our hair and hope we didn't look too sleepy.

It was Maggie. "Stefan and I brought all the presents down from my room, and we're ready to open them in the lobby."

When we got there, we saw Birdie Lancaster sitting on a folding chair. A platter heaped with her scrumptious chocolate chip cookies sat on the coffee table, and Ivy brought a tray loaded with coffee cups. The kids were arranging presents and cards on two tables they had brought from the kitchen. Soon all the hotel guests were gathered in the area, and Asbury, Ivy, and David stood to the side. Ward and Willard came in and stood beside them. Franz and Erika insisted that Andrea and I sit on the chairs by the fireplace. Eva rushed in at the last minute and sat down on the one remaining folding chair, beside Erika.

"Why don't you and Stefan sit on the couch," Andrea said, "and David can bring the presents to you?"

This worked out well, and soon we all were sipping coffee, munching cookies, and watching as the kids opened presents. They hadn't registered for gifts anywhere; obviously if you live in a hotel and eat all your meals out or on hotel china, there really isn't much call for toasters and blenders. However, they did get one of each, and they both graciously acted pleased about them. They opened our present right away—a gift certificate for Amazon that Andrea had ordered online. It was the most appropriate gift we could think of, considering the kids' circumstances.

The most interesting gifts were from their friends at the ski school and Maggie's college companions. Some had gone together to get them a copy of *"Appalachian Trail Thru-Hikers Companion,"* and another book that was a hit featured the trees of the Allegheny Mountains. Then there were several items that I figured must be ski equipment, and some great-looking gloves for skiing. They both looked pleased, or maybe I should say overwhelmed, by a bulky envelope from Franz and Erika, but they didn't say what was in it. I was dying of curiosity, but they went on to the next package. Laszlo had put together an album of old family photos, and I hoped to get a chance to go through it later.

Near the end, Maggie opened Eva's present. It was something in a frame; we could only see the back of it as she held it for Stefan to look at. She smiled sweetly at Eva and said, "Thank you so much, Eva. I'm sure this will bring back memories for Stefan."

She handed it to me so we could pass it around, and I saw it was a photo of Stefan and Eva as teenagers, standing together in front of a snowy mountain with their arms around each other's waists. They were wearing ski clothes. I smiled and nodded as if this were a typical wedding gift; I wasn't about to give Eva the satisfaction of thinking she had upset any of us, especially since Maggie handled the situation so well.

Finally all the gifts had been opened and exclaimed over, and David and Asbury helped Maggie and Stefan carry everything to her room. We went to our room to repair our makeup and wait for the kids to be ready to go to dinner.

"What do you suppose was in that envelope from Franz and Erika?" I asked.

"I have no idea, but I have a feeling we'll find out soon."

"Do you think they'll tell us at dinner?"

"I think they might." She put the finishing touches on her lipstick.

"What do you think of that picture Eva gave them? Or I should say, what do you think of the picture she gave Stefan?"

"Most unusual and not at all appropriate. She's blatant about her interest in Stefan, even though he discourages it."

"Maggie handles the situation well, I think."

Andrea started to answer, but someone knocked on the door at that moment. It was Maggie. "Stefan's opening the car. We're starving."

"We could have taken the Accord," Andrea said.

"That's okay. We know where it is."

Stefan drove the Volvo, and Andrea and I relaxed in the backseat. Before we knew it we arrived at Muttley's, a charming and unique place. We all ordered iced tea and browsed through menus. "Willard says the steak is good here," I said.

"It is," Stefan said. "Let's all have some."

When we had ordered and were sipping our tea, Maggie said, "I explained to Stefan about the flower garden and the foxglove, and how Isabelle saw a woman out there the night of the wedding."

Stefan frowned. "It probably doesn't mean anything. Anyway, I knew Amalie loves flowers, so I emailed her weeks ago about Maggie's garden. I sent her a photo and told her about all the plants growing there. That may have been her that Isabelle saw. I'm sure she just went out to see the garden."

When it was almost dark? She would have had plenty of opportunity to see the garden in broad daylight in the time before the wedding. I didn't say anything about this, though, or the fact that Amalie's a pharmacy student.

"The girls are like sisters to me," he said. "Being an only child, I've always felt exceptionally close to them. Neither of them is capable of murder; of that I'm positive."

Well, the thought was out in the open. But this was an intimate dinner, not a criminal investigation, and I tried to think of another more appropriate subject. "The girls seem very nice, and they're having a good time getting to know David."

Stefan laughed. "David's having a good time hanging out with two older women. Especially foreign women. He's never had it so good."

"It's going to be a real letdown for him when they leave," Andrea said.

"I'll keep him busy helping on the attic. He's a pretty good worker. I think I'll give him a raise—he's been saving up for a lot of new ski equipment."

Maggie looked thoughtful, as if trying to figure out how to impart big news. "We wanted to let you know what Stefan's folks gave us. They own a chalet at Innsbruck, and they're in the process of deeding it to us. We're thinking it would be a wonderful place for big family get-togethers. Maybe we can all spend the Christmas holidays there this winter."

"What a wonderful gift!" Andrea said.

My first thought was that I was going to have to fly to get there, but I'd put off thinking about that. "Yes, that's truly a wonderful gift."

Our steaks arrived, and we forgot about everything else. They were delicious. Everyone else said no to dessert, so I did, too, and we finished our tea and started back to the hotel. After thanking the kids and telling them goodnight, we went to our room.

I spoke softly, since their room was directly overhead. "What do you think of that? Amalie knew about the foxglove before they came to the valley. And why would she be out there in the dark if she wanted to see the garden? Wouldn't she have gone out in the daylight? Then there's also this— Nicole is out of the room so much, talking with David outside our window, that she'd never know what Amalie might be up to."

Andrea merely looked thoughtful, as usual. "I'm sure time will tell us who killed Laszlo and John."

And as usual, I couldn't help wondering whether Andrea knew more than she was telling me.

CHAPTER ELEVEN

Someone knocked on our door before we were even out of bed. Andrea put on her robe and opened the door. "Good morning."

"Good morning. Sorry if I woke you, but we were ready to go out to breakfast, and we wondered if you'd like to go to Elkins with us today. We're going to the Tygart Valley Mall."

I recognized the voice as Claudia's. "I'm game if you are," I said from the bed. Who knew what we might find out if we spent some time with the sisters? And I was even willing to put up with Claudia's negativity if it meant going to a mall I'd never visited before.

"We'd like to go with you," Andrea said. "What time are you leaving?"

"We thought about ten. We can get something to eat there later."

"Good. We'll see you in the lobby at ten."

We got ready for the day and went to the lobby. Ivy was behind the desk, as usual. "I think I heard Ms. Martin inviting you to go to Elkins. If you want some breakfast here, there's still some cereal in the kitchen and a little milk. Help yourselves. It needs to be eaten up. There's coffee in there, too."

We thanked Ivy and went to the kitchen, where we sat at the small table in the corner with coffee and Cheerios. "I'm not sure why they're determined to invite us out, but who knows, we might find out something useful," I said.

"That's entirely possible. I'll ask Maggie and Stefan if we can bring them anything. There's probably a Sears there, and maybe a Penneys."

She went up the attic stairs when she finished, thinking she'd find the kids working in the attic, and I washed up and went back to the lobby. "Do you have any guests checking in today?" I asked.

Ivy looked at her computer screen. "Not till tomorrow. We have some couples coming for the weekend. Thank goodness, it's been quiet for a couple of days now. I think it would be bad for the hotel's reputation to have yellow tape stretched around and deputies everywhere. People would begin asking questions."

"Yes, we don't want anything that would be bad for business here. Have they taken down the tape from Laszlo's and John's doors?"

"Yes, it's down, thank goodness."

It suddenly occurred to me that we hadn't investigated John's room. I'd have to mention it to Andrea when she came down. And it wasn't long before she came from the kitchen. "Maggie and Stefan don't need anything. They certainly seem to be well-organized."

"That's fine. We'll just enjoy browsing in the mall. Do you realize we haven't checked out John Fuller's room to see what we can find in there?"

"I've been thinking about it. We've been so busy concentrating on Laszlo, since he was Stefan's uncle, that I've neglected the other room. We'll go in there tomorrow. Ward said they took all his things to check and then send to his family, if family can be located. The reason they left Laszlo's things here after checking them was because they'll go to Franz to dispose of."

Just then the sisters walked in, looking like they'd just stepped out of a fashion magazine. Both were in dark pant suits, and their hair and nails made me wonder if they'd been to a salon rather than to breakfast. Both were in moderately high heels, wearing hose.

I had put on a pair of polyester pants that morning and an acrylic cardigan over a polyester blouse. The valley was a good place for layering. Andrea was wearing jeans and sneakers. She looked totally comfortable with what she had on, and it was obvious that she wasn't considering changing.

"It's a little early, but we might as well get started if you're ready," Claudia said.

"I'll get our purses," Andrea said, and started toward our room.

Agnes was smiling. "This will be fun. A shopping spree."

"I'm looking forward to it," I said. *And hoping you or Claudia will say something that will be a clue to the killer in our midst.*

Andrea returned with both purses, and we all got into the sisters' rental car. Again, I found myself searching for something to talk about, while Andrea, beside me in the backseat, seemed perfectly satisfied to say nothing and gaze at the scenery. And the scenery proved to be the main topic of conversation all the way to Elkins.

When we reached the town, Claudia drove directly to the mall. They must have been there before, I figured. Well, it beat driving all over and searching and stopping to ask directions and searching some more. They'd probably done that on their first trip and gotten it out of the way.

We spent the rest of the morning looking in smaller shops, sometimes getting lost from each other, then searching up and down and getting reconnected. "Keep your cell phone on," Andrea told me. "At least I can call you if we get separated." She turned to Claudia. "I guess you and Agnes have European numbers, and I couldn't call them."

"That's right," Claudia said. "Let's plan to meet in the food court at one, and we can have some lunch and reassemble. That way we can go our separate ways if we want."

We all walked along in the same general direction, stopping at shop windows and sometimes going in until finally I didn't know where anyone else was. No problem, though. I was wearing my watch, and I'd find the food court and the others at one. Then I did run into Claudia as she was coming out of a nail shop. "I broke a nail and was able to get it fixed in there," she said.

So that explained those gorgeous fingernails of hers. They were fake. I looked at my own short unpolished nails and stubby fingers. They did the job for me—washing dishes, cleaning, quilting, and gardening. Yet I admit there were times when I longed for a more glamorous look. "Your nails don't come off in water?"

"No, they're permanent, at least until I want to make a change. Or occasionally I break one. Of course, I don't have my hands in water that often." She looked at her watch. "It's almost one. We'd better go to the food court and find the others."

She struck out toward the food court, and I had to hurry to keep up. Andrea and Agnes were standing beside a vacant table when we got there, and they motioned to us. I wanted to ask Claudia more about her nails, but we got involved in checking out the offerings and deciding what we wanted. Andrea has no use for vanity, and I'm sure she would consider fake nails a terribly vain thing, so that wouldn't have been a good topic of conversation anyway. Then I had a vision of digging around in my garden with such nails, and I knew they'd never work for me.

We settled on salads and soon were eating and discussing the morning's purchases. At least Claudia and Agnes were. Andrea and I hadn't bought anything. Both of the sisters had bought sweaters, which they brought out of their bags to show us. They looked like wool, and here I was in my acrylic cardigan. There's not a lot of call for high fashion in Pine Summit.

We split up after eating and agreed to meet back at the food court at three for coffee before the trip back to the hotel. I still hadn't been able to think of anything to say that would get the sisters talking about something that would help in solving the murders. Not that I thought they knew anything about them—I had firmly decided Amalie was the guilty one. It's just that you never know when a chance remark will lead to expanded knowledge.

Andrea and I started out together, but I soon lost her in the Sears. I decided to look at clothes, thinking I'd find some nice cotton pants that would be more up-to-date than my polyester ones. Andrea wandered off somewhere, and I never saw her after that. I looked all over the store for her, but she was nowhere to be found. We'd meet up at three, I figured, and paid for a pair of pants and an all-cotton shirt I found. And by the time three o'clock came around, my feet were tired and I was ready to sit down for coffee.

I got to the food court first, and then Andrea showed up. In just a few minutes the sisters came in together, loaded with packages. "How will you get all your purchases home?" I asked.

"We always travel with two bags—one full and one empty for the things we buy," Claudia said.

No one was hungry, so we had coffee and started back to the hotel. "Thanks very much for asking us. It was a pleasant day," Andrea said when we were getting out of the car.

"Yes, thanks a bunch. It was fun," I said.

"It was our pleasure," Agnes said.

We went to our room, where I plopped down on my bed. "Nap time!"

"I agree. My feet are tired."

We had barely dozed off when we heard voices from Franz and Erika's room next door. Were they arguing again? What was it this time? Andrea went to our door and opened it a crack. She's normally not a nosy person, but when murders have been committed, she's all ears.

"Can you hear what they're saying?" I whispered.

"Not if you keep talking." The voices stopped, and Andrea came back to bed. "I heard Laszlo's name a few times, but that's all I could make out. Possibly it was about money again. Or an even remoter possibility is that it was about Erika's relationship with Laszlo."

"That was years ago."

"I suspect that spouses seem to accept things sometimes, but they fester and erupt years later during a time of stress."

I didn't question Andrea's ability to talk about what spouses do, even though she's never had one. She's the analytical one with an uncanny ability to size up situations. "Do you think she's a spendthrift, and that results in their arguments? Or is he a tightwad?"

"She does do a lot of shopping. That probably doesn't mean anything, though. Maybe it's the stress of the murders that sends her on those shopping sprees."

"I wonder if Stefan knows they argue so much."

"He probably does. I don't think it's anything serious. Even the stress of traveling to a foreign country and attending your only son's wedding could set some people off."

"Where do you want to eat tonight?"

She got up and went to the window. "I noticed some clouds moving in, and now it's started to drizzle. Let's just pick up a sandwich somewhere and eat by the fire. I'll go get some sandwiches right now, before it starts raining any harder, if you want to go on napping."

"You don't mind?"

"Of course not." She took her purse and got a jacket from the closet. "I'll be back shortly."

Andrea probably was hoping for an excuse to get some time to herself. She's always been somewhat of a loner.

I got up after dozing and washed my face, trying to wake up. Andrea came in with sandwiches, a bag of decaf coffee, and a box of hot chocolate packets. "It's a good night for something hot to drink with the food," she said.

We went to the lobby where Maggie was behind the desk. She had taken over the evening shift, giving Ivy a chance to spend the evenings at home. Andrea went to the kitchen to start a pot of decaf. I went to the desk. "Have you had something to eat?"

"Stefan's bringing sandwiches. Andrea asked me earlier. It's kind of dreary to go out."

Stefan arrived with sandwiches, and Andrea came from the kitchen with coffee on a tray. Someone had built a fire and we sat around it. "What are your folks doing tonight?" I asked Stefan.

"I think they went out. They asked if we wanted to go, but we decided to stay in. It would have meant asking Ivy to work late, and she's done more than her share of that lately."

About that time the sisters came from their room, and Claudia said, "What a good idea! A picnic! Where did you get the sandwiches?"

Andrea directed her to the nearby Canaan Valley Store, and they left. "I'll refill our cups and put on another pot," I said. "It's decaf, so we can have all we want."

I supposed Stefan was right, that his parents had gone out, and the Beckers never showed up. The sisters returned, and the six of us sat around chatting and enjoying the fire, gradually changing over from coffee to a cup of hot chocolate. Even Claudia was in a pleasant mood, and she concentrated on asking the kids about their honeymoon.

When we finally got to our room, I looked out the window. "It's raining harder out there. Tomorrow will be a perfect day to stay in and investigate John Fuller's room. People may be checking in for the weekend, and we want to get through before someone takes that room"

We heard Franz and Erika come in and close their door, and then all was quiet. "Sounds like we're going to have a quiet night tonight," I said.

Andrea shoved the chair under the doorknob and locked the door. "Let's hope it's not the calm before the storm."

#

Andrea had finished her book. She's usually prepared with enough books, but we had stayed in the Canaan Valley longer than we planned. She asked Stefan if she could borrow something from his library, thinking he would have something interesting, and he gave her his key. I followed her upstairs to his room.

Andrea pulled a thin paperback from the bookshelf and was riffling through it. "I saw this and noticed it was by someone named Eva, and I instantly thought of Eva Weiss. It's a book of poetry by someone named Eva Jung. It was published ten years ago, probably by a self-publisher. It's in German."

"It could be Eva Weiss. Maybe that's her maiden name."

"Even if it is, it's not proof she wrote the poem we found. As far as we know, she had no reason in the world to kill two people." She put the book back. "Here's *Walden*. I haven't read any Thoreau in years. I'll take this."

"Someone returned the keys," Ivy said when we went back downstairs.

I stood there looking at her, not sure what she meant. "You mean . . ."

"Someone returned the extra room keys, the ones that were missing."

"Oh. I wonder when that happened."

"I don't know. I hadn't looked in there in a couple of days. But they're back this morning."

"Do you have a safe back there?"

"There's one under the desk. I don't know the combination, though."

I thought about this, wishing that Andrea would come from our room, where she had taken the book, and figure out what to say next. "Does Stefan know they're back?"

"I tried to call him on his cell phone, but he didn't answer. I definitely think we should start keeping them in the safe now."

"I'm sure Stefan and Maggie will agree. We were just in his room, borrowing a book for Andrea. They weren't there, but I haven't heard any pounding from upstairs. I'll check Maggie's room."

I climbed the stairs and knocked on Maggie's door, and Stefan answered right away. I could see behind him that they were putting books from Maggie's bookcase into boxes. "Ivy was trying to call you. She says the keys have been returned."

"The missing keys? The spare ones?"

"Yes. She said they're back in the drawer."

"I'll call the sheriff. They'll want to check for fingerprints."

I went back downstairs to find Ivy and Andrea talking about the keys. "Stefan's calling the sheriff so he can come and check for fingerprints."

"It's still raining," Ivy said. "Asbury went out and got a bunch of Danish so anyone who doesn't want to go out can have breakfast here."

"Wonderful!" Andrea said. "Do you think I should put on the big coffee pot?"

"I already started it. It should be ready by now."

We were just settled in the kitchen when the Beckers came in. They sat at the table next to us. "Did you enjoy your visit to Blackwater Falls?" Andrea asked.

"Very much so. We spent the whole day there. We were all tired when we got home."

They seemed like such an average family, in spite of Nicole's somewhat rambunctious demeanor. But there was something about Amalie, I was sure of it. She was just too quiet. She seemed like the type who would write poetry, and I was betting she had written the poem we found in the dumpster. Then I happened to think that people who didn't know Andrea might be suspicious of her under similar circumstances. She's just as quiet and introspective as Amalie.

The Beckers finished their rolls and left, going to their rooms, I supposed. "That Amalie, she's just too quiet. You know what they say—it's always the quiet ones."

Andrea laughed. "I don't think you can categorize people that way."

"What about the fact that she was seen at the flower garden, picking something, on the night Laszlo died?"

"Number one, we don't know it was her. And if it was, maybe she enjoys gardens in the moonlight. After all, there was a full moon that night."

"But Isabelle said she was picking something. Would she take the liberty of picking flowers in Maggie's garden?"

Our niece walked in. "What about Maggie's garden?"

"There's coffee and Danish," Andrea said. "We were talking about what Isabelle said, that she saw someone in your flower garden on the night of the wedding. Did Amalie or anyone ask you if it would be okay to pick flowers from the garden?"

"No one asked me or even mentioned the garden."

"I wonder if Hadley ever saw flowers in the girls' room when she was cleaning it," Andrea said. "I'll ask her when I see her."

Maggie went to the coffeepot and filled a cup. "I've talked to everyone now who stayed in that end of the hotel on the night of the wedding. No one else saw anything. It was only Isabelle."

"It's important that she did. The only problem is that every woman in the family, and Claudia and Agnes, too, was wearing a light-colored, summery dress that evening. It could have been any of the women."

Maggie helped herself to a Danish, too. "I wouldn't dream of mentioning this to Stefan, but I think the fact that Klaus is a pharmacist and Amalie is a pharmacy student is rather suspicious, too. Stefan's really attached to everyone in his family, and he can't believe any one of them would commit a murder. Of course, Agnes is like one of the family, too, since she lived with them for so long and followed the family from one diplomatic post to another."

Suddenly, I couldn't resist asking: "Do Stefan's parents argue a lot?"

Andrea took a deep breath, almost as if part of her wished I hadn't said it and part was glad I did.

"Stefan says they always have. They're crazy about each other, but they have these blowups at times. Have you heard them arguing?"

"A couple of times," Andrea said. "These are naturally stressful times for them, and it's easy to see that if they have that kind of relationship, they would be prone to arguing now."

Maggie finished her Danish. "I have to go help Stefan. He's determined to continue work on the attic in spite of murders, visiting relatives, and whatever else might happen."

"We'll clean up the dishes. We're going to check out John Fuller's room to see if anything interesting can be found in there," I said.

"Good luck. I think the deputies totally cleaned out everything and took it with them, but knowing my aunts, there's going to be some clue left behind that you'll discover."

When we got back to the lobby, a deputy was there behind the desk, bagging up the spare keys. Stefan was with him, and when the deputy left, Stefan began showing Ivy the combination to the safe. We sat down by the fireplace, which someone had lit the fire in this morning due to the rain. When Stefan was through and went back upstairs, Andrea asked Ivy, "Is Hadley here this morning?"

"She's cleaning your room right now."

We went on back to our room, and Hadley said, "Do you want me to clear out? I'm almost through now."

"No," Andrea said. "We have a question for you. Have you ever seen any flowers from Maggie's garden in any of the rooms?"

"I hope I'm not getting anyone in trouble for picking flowers, but I noticed some in the girls' room. You know, the Becker girls."

"Could you tell what kind they were?"

"I don't know the name, but they're kinda bell-shaped. I think they were yellow and pink."

"Thanks, Hadley. That answers my question. And no, you didn't get anyone in trouble."

We went back to the desk. "Is the John Fuller room unlocked?" Andrea asked.

Ivy looked up from the safe, where she was trying the combination. "Probably not. I put some people in there this morning. Is that a problem?"

"No, not a problem. We were going to check out the room, but I imagine the deputies found everything, anyway. How long will they be here?"

"Through the weekend. It's a couple with a little boy. I put them all the way back there in case he's noisy. He won't disturb the rest of you that way. Stefan and David brought one of the rollaway beds down for him."

How they'd find room for another bed in the hotel's small rooms, I couldn't imagine. "We'll check it out when they leave. Even if there's something there, they wouldn't know its significance and probably would ignore it."

We sat by the fire and were trying to figure out what to do with ourselves on a rainy day when Eva Weiss came through the door. She was wearing a red jacket, and her blonde hair was pulled back, showing off her perfect face. She looked radiant, I had to admit. "Is Stefan here? And Maggie?"

It was as if she were adding Maggie as an afterthought. "They're up in the attic, framing a room. They're turning the attic into a third floor with more rooms for guests." Somehow, I couldn't see Miss Perfect framing a room. She had perfect fingernails just as Claudia had, and I hoped a fungus was growing under them.

"I'll go check with Franz and Erika. It's such a dreary day, I thought it would be fun to go to brunch somewhere. It would do them both good to get out of their room."

She was gone for quite a while, and eventually the three of them came into the lobby. "Good morning," Erika said. "We're just going out to brunch, if they're still serving breakfast at the lodge. Would you two like to go with us?" Eva had the look of an expert poker player at that moment. She hadn't anticipated Erika's asking us to go along.

"Thanks, but we ate already," Andrea said. "Have a good time. I think we're going to read here in front of the fire and hope it clears up before lunch."

We had barely settled down to read when we heard someone in the hallway, and a small child came scooting along, pushing a wooden truck that was almost as big as he was. He made truck noises all around the lobby. "Oh, dear," I said. "It may not be as peaceful as we'd like." Unfortunately, there wasn't room to read in our room, unless we wanted to read in bed.

"Why don't you take your truck back to your room?" Ivy asked.

"No!" he shouted and continued rumbling around the lobby.

"Some people don't do anything to control their children," I said. "He should be taught some manners."

Andrea was simply watching him and his truck. She walked over to him. "What's your name?"

"Jason."

"Can I see your truck?"

"No!"

Andrea reached down and picked up the truck, and Jason started screaming. "Get a plastic bag from the kitchen," she yelled above the screams.

"What is it?" I asked on the way to the kitchen.

"The knife."

"Oh my God! The knife that killed John Fuller," I yelled as I rushed away to the kitchen.

CHAPTER TWELVE

The lobby was chaotic when I came back from the kitchen. Jason's parents were there, yelling at Andrea for taking his truck and making him cry. She was totally unconcerned, and held the truck up where he couldn't reach it. She lowered it when she saw me with the plastic bag, and I opened it. She picked up the knife from the bed of the truck by the sides of the blade and placed it carefully into the bag.

Jason's mother gasped and sat down on the couch. The lobby was suddenly very quiet. "What the hell?" the father said.

Andrea was on the phone to Ward, and I was thinking it would be necessary to explain to these guests that a murder had been committed in their room. Not years ago, which might result in a fascinating ghost roaming the hallways, but just days ago. I stood there, wondering just how to go about it, when Andrea hung up the phone. "There was a murder in your room recently. The murder weapon hadn't been located, but somehow your son seems to have found it."

Jason was huddled against his mother, and Andrea turned to him. "Jason, can you show me where you found the knife?"

"No!"

"The sheriff's on his way, and he'll need to talk to Jason."

Maybe the uniform will impress the little brat enough so that he'll talk, I thought. The husband sat down on the couch beside his wife, and they started discussing demanding their money back and checking out. Maggie and Stefan appeared from the kitchen; they had come down the attic stairs. "What's all the noise?" Stefan asked.

Andrea explained the situation to him, and the couple went to him and asked for a refund. "No problem," he said, and went with them to the desk, where he did whatever it took to get a credit issued to them.

Willard walked in and immediately went up to Jason. He leaned down and picked him up, and Jason smiled angelically. "Let's go to your room. I want you to show me where you found that knife."

I decided right then and there that Willard would make a good stepfather, as he chatted with Jason while carrying him down the hall. The parents trailed after him, and Stefan, Andrea and I brought up the rear. We weren't about to be left out. We wanted to know where that knife had been found. Willard set Jason down in the middle of the crowded room, and the boy ran to the window. He pulled the curtain back and pointed to the lining. "There," he said.

Meanwhile, the parents were packing up and getting ready to leave. The mother started wiping down the truck with an antiseptic wipe. The father grabbed Jason's hand. "Let's go." He had a suitcase in the other hand, and Jason's mom was carrying another one.

"Just a minute," Willard said.

"You can't hold us here. We're leaving. They have our address and phone number at the desk. If you need anything, you can call us." They walked out.

Jason started screaming again as his father dragged him down the hall. "I wanna see the man's gun!" He was still screaming as they went out the front door.

We all looked at the lining of the curtain where the knife had been inserted through a slit, then went back to the lobby, and Andrea handed the plastic bag to Willard. "Thanks for taking care of the evidence," he said. "I feel sure the fingerprints have been wiped off, but we'll check the dried blood against Fuller's." Then he hesitated only a moment before saying, "You wouldn't have any coffee would you? And some more of that wedding cake?"

I could hardly keep from laughing. A serial killer could slay dozens, but eating would always be uppermost in Willard's mind. "I'll go put on the coffee." The cake was beginning to get a little dried out, in spite of the plastic container we'd put it in, so maybe it would be a good thing if we let Willard eat all he wanted. They followed me into the kitchen.

Maggie and Stefan joined us, and we had hardly gotten started when the sheriff came in. Andrea explained the situation to him as she poured coffee for him and gave him a piece of cake. I took cake and coffee to Ivy, and that left only enough for two pieces. I put them in a small container to be delivered to Asbury and David.

The sheriff hadn't seemed unduly disturbed when Andrea and I found evidence previously, and he didn't act that way now that a three-year-old had found a knife missed by his deputies. After all, who would think to look in the drapery lining? The sheriff is a true stoic, a perfect match for Andrea. Or maybe they're too much alike. Maybe they'd be bored with each other. Whatever, they didn't seem to be making much progress in the romance department. Of course, being in the middle of investigating two murders can put a damper on romance.

The others gradually finished up and left to get back to work. "Let's finish the coffee, and then we'll go give that room a thorough investigation," Andrea said.

I poured the last bit into our cups. "That's the last of the wedding cake, and about time. It was a little stale."

"Unlike the kids' marriage. They seem totally wrapped up in each other."

"Thank goodness. That nasty Eva could create problems for them, otherwise."

"She is rather frank about her interest in Stefan, isn't she? Not much to be done about that, I guess, since she lives just down the road."

I got up and took the cups and plates to the sink to wash. "Do you suppose she has money? She has no visible means of support, and yet she dresses in expensive clothes and her grooming's something else. She looks as if she went to the salon every day."

Andrea started drying dishes. "She may have whopping credit card bills, too, and no way to pay them." We finished, and she went into the laundry room and got the downstairs vacuum cleaner. "We'll find more dust, I'm sure, so we might as well take care of it. Get the box of plastic bags, please, just in case."

We passed Ivy on the way and explained what we were doing. "Hadley just cleaned that room before those people came," she said.

"We move the furniture to check everything," Andrea said. "You know there's always some dust under the furniture, so we might as well clean it up while we're at it."

"I'll admit, I rarely moved the furniture and cleaned under it when I was doing the cleaning."

"That would be a spring cleaning," I said. "You'd never get through if you did that every day."

"Good luck. If there's anything else there, I hope you find it. I'll be glad when this investigation's over and things get back to normal around here."

Maggie and Stefan had already moved the rollaway bed to wherever they kept those, so that would make it easier to move things around. This room had the standard arrangement—two twin beds separated by a nightstand, and a chest opposite. That was it. I was beginning to like the idea of such spare accommodations, being in a beautiful, natural place like the Canaan Valley. Such a room would never go over in Charleston, or any other city. People would be screaming for a television and phone. Well, at least a television. Everyone has a cell phone these days.

The side windows looked out onto the adjacent vacant lot—vacant, that is, except for Maggie's flower garden. The flowers looked beautiful in the morning sunshine, belying their deadly potential. I opened the curtains as wide as they'd go to give us more light.

We moved the chest first, and I went through the drawers while Andrea inspected the floor and ran the vacuum cleaner. The drawers were totally empty, without a speck of dust. "Hadley's done a good job of cleaning," I said.

"Yes, the room looks nice. Let's put the chest back"

We moved one of the beds to the side and followed the same procedure. We even moved the mattress, but there was nothing under it. Next came the nightstand, and in the drawer I found a brochure touting the attractions of the valley. I looked through it carefully to see if anything had been written in it but found nothing. Andrea's investigative techniques were rubbing off on me.

As we started to move the second bed, Andrea stopped and got down on her knees. She began pulling at something that seemed to be imbedded in the carpet. "What is it?" I asked.

"Not sure. Just a minute." She got up and went to the window, holding something tiny in her fingers. "It's part of a fingernail."

"Good. They can check it for DNA."

"It's undoubtedly fake."

"Oh. When we were in Elkins with the sisters, at the mall, and we were all separated, I was coming out of one of the stores. I saw Claudia coming from the nail place, and she said she had broken a fingernail and was having it fixed."

"That's interesting."

"I'm still sure it's Amalie who committed the murders," I whispered. We were in their end of the hotel. "Does she have fake nails?"

"Both the girls have beautiful nails, but I'm not sure if they're fake or not. But both the sisters do, and I think Eva does, too."

"I could see the sisters as suspects, but what reason could Eva have to kill two people?"

Andrea put the fingernail fragment in a plastic bag. "Nothing is clear at present. And this fingernail may mean nothing. It could have been here for years, the way it was imbedded in the carpet. And even if it belongs to someone here, it doesn't mean they're guilty of murder. It only means they were in this room."

Andrea's so darned logical and rational that I wonder at times if she has any imagination. We moved the bed, and there was nothing under it. Andrea ran the vacuum cleaner, and we lifted the mattress. There we found a piece of paper. I picked it up, by the edge, of course. "It's another poem." I read:

> "Spoiler
> You took it all and left nothing
> Bereft, without what I need
> But there is justice to be had
> With the thrust of a blade"

"Good Lord! That could hardly be more specific," Andrea said.

Rarely does Andrea speak in exclamations, so I knew this shook her. It shook me, too. "Who would be most likely to write a poem? And why would someone write poems to their victims?"

Andrea shook her head. "She wanted them to be frightened before they were killed. A little added revenge. Or maybe there's another reason. No telling."

"You say 'she.' Can we be sure it's a woman?"

"Poisoning is reputed to be a woman's crime. And the poems seem like something a woman would write. Then in addition, it was a woman Isabelle saw in the flower garden on the night of the wedding."

"But the knife looked like a hunting knife—something a man would be more likely to have."

"That's true. There's still a lot to be learned about these murders."

We put the poem in a bag and put the room back together. When we went to the lobby, Ivy wanted to see what was in our bags, and she exclaimed over the poem, too. "Good grief, that's gruesome."

"I think it's time to go to lunch. I'll call Ward and see if he can meet us at the lodge so we can give him these things." Andrea pulled out her cell phone and called Ward, then told me, "He's at Davis right now. We'll meet him at Blackwater."

We put away the vacuum cleaner and box of plastic bags, got our purses, and took off for the Blackwater Lodge, hoping for a relaxing and peaceful lunch after the morning's shocks.

#

Ward was just driving into the parking lot at the lodge when we arrived. Andrea gave him the bags, and he locked them in the trunk of his car. We went through the lobby and into the restaurant. "We're not finding fingerprints on anything, as expected," he said.

"I suppose the killer was very careful and wiped everything, or possibly wore gloves," I said.

"With gloves, there probably would be other people's prints on the evidence. When the items have been wiped thoroughly, there aren't any prints at all."

The waitress came and we all ordered iced tea and started looking at the menus. It would be salads, as usual, I was sure.

In spite of my tremendous appetite, I do try to stay healthy. After we'd ordered, Ward looked at Andrea. "Your suggestion seems to be working."

"Which one is that?" she asked.

"About the acetone."

I was dying to know what they were talking about and hoping that if I just kept quiet long enough, I'd find out.

I must have had a quizzical expression, because the sheriff turned to me. "Andrea suggested we soak that phone memory card in acetone. It's dissolving the glue, or whatever was on it. We're hoping it won't damage the card so much that we can't tell what's in the memory."

"What would be on it, except for the phone numbers in what Andrea tells me is a phone book?"

"It'll show outgoing and incoming calls, as well as the numbers the owner had stored in the phone. We hope to be able to tell who he talked to last, and at what time, before he died. This is assuming he hadn't deleted those calls."

"I suppose it's possible the killer deleted everything from the memory card," Andrea said, "but why would they have bothered putting the glue on it if that were the case?"

"Maybe they thought it would be simpler to dunk it in glue and be done with it."

It irritated me that he didn't seem to find it surprising Andrea hadn't explained her idea about the acetone to me, but I didn't show it. As a matter of fact, I was surprised the sheriff was explaining it. They're a pair of closed-mouth types, for sure.

I couldn't resist asking, "Andrea, what made you think of acetone?"

"Since there are so many women around who appear to have fake nails, I thought about the glue that's used to hold them on. I wondered if someone had used the nail glue to disable the phone card, so I checked on the Internet and found that acetone is used to remove them."

"Our technical wizard is working on it this morning," Ward said. "There's one in every sheriff's department these days, you know. The man's useless with a revolver, can't hit the broad side of a barn, but give him anything electronic and he can figure it out."

"That's an important asset to any law enforcement agency," I said, thinking I'd be useless with electronics or a gun. "Did Andrea tell you about Claudia Martin having a broken nail repaired at the mall?"

"Yes, she told me."

The waitress brought our salads—I was surprised Ward had ordered one, too, but he does have a fine physique for a man his age. We started telling him about the work Maggie and Stefan were doing in the attic of the hotel, and that they were hoping to have more rooms ready for ski season. It was a relief to talk about something beside murder, and I found myself relaxing and enjoying the lunch. We'd get back to the hotel and start thinking about the murders again, but for now, it was time to relax.

As we were leaving, Ward said, "We've checked both those rental cars over thoroughly. I gave them another look this morning when I was at the hotel. They could be returned, if someone can arrange to get them back to the airport." He smiled at Andrea. "I removed the seats and checked the spare tire compartment. The glove compartment, too. And I looked under the floor mats."

It was interesting to me that Ward thought of saving money for the estates of two men who obviously were rolling in it by having their rental cars returned.

"If Maggie and Stefan can take a day off tomorrow, I'll follow them to Charleston and bring them back," Andrea said.

"It would do them good to take a day off from all the construction in the attic," I said.

#

As soon as we walked into the Alpenhof, Andrea said, "I'm going to use Stefan's computer."

"What are you looking up this time?"

"I want to see whether Eva Weiss was one of the investors in Laszlo and John's venture that lost everyone money."

"I don't know why you're interested in her. She obviously has money, or she wouldn't be living here where rents are fairly high, not working or showing any signs she might go to work, and really has no motive for killing anybody—except maybe Maggie, that is." I said this with a little laugh, letting

152

Andrea know I was joking, but I still wished I hadn't said it as soon as the words popped out of my mouth.

I continued, "By the way, I've changed my mind about who did it. Forget Amalie—now I'm sure it was Claudia. She's the one who had the broken nail, and she's a mean, negative person. Seems to me she's capable of murder."

Andrea was looking as if she were lost in thought and not hearing a word I was saying. "How old would you say Eva is?"

"I don't know. If she and Stefan were in school together, I'd say she's his age, twenty-seven. Why?"

"Just trying to figure things out. I'm going to get Stefan's key." She started up the stairs, and I was torn between spending a boring hour in Stefan's room or getting my book and reading by the fire. I could put on coffee, have cookies with Ivy . . . it all sounded appealing, but I followed Andrea instead.

She knocked on Stefan's door, but there was no response. "They must be in the attic. I'll go around and go up the attic stairs. Have a seat on the bench, and I'll be back in no time."

I sighed and sat down. The prospect of reading by the fire, coffee, and cookies was becoming more appealing by the minute. I stayed put, however. I must admit, I was curious about what Andrea might find. She came back shortly, unlocked the door, and we went in.

"I suppose they'll be turning Maggie's room into another guest room," I said.

Andrea sat down at the computer and turned it on. "I'm wondering whether they have room in here for all her things. They both have a lot of books. Clothes, not so many, but even so his closet looks like it would be too small."

It took her no time at all to come up with the web site she was looking for. She must have remembered from her previous researching. "There's no Eva Weiss here."

She took out her cell phone and punched some buttons. "Ask Stefan what Eva's father's name is, please." She waited. "Kurt Jung. Thanks. Oh, I just wanted to check something."

She hung up. "If Eva's twenty-seven, she could have been a minor when the financial disaster took place. I'll check on her father."

"Why didn't you ask that when you were up there?"

"I didn't want Stefan to know I was checking on Eva unless I had to. They've known each other for years, and I'm sure he doesn't think she's capable of murder, just as he doesn't think his family members are."

"Well, someone is. Do you see Kurt Jung there?"

"No, but there's a Gertrude Jung. Oh, dear. I wish I'd asked about the mother, too."

There are times when it's rather refreshing to see evidence that Andrea isn't always perfect in every way. "Call her again."

"I'll have to." More button-pushing. "What was her mother's name? Gertrude. Thanks." She snapped the phone shut. "That book of poetry in Stefan's bookcase undoubtedly was written by Eva Weiss. Of course, it doesn't mean she's guilty. It just means she writes poetry, and that causes suspicion to mount."

So another suspect could be added to the long list. I kept changing my mind about who was guilty, and now the picture seemed more muddled than ever. "Maybe it was Agnes, or Karla Becker, and we're just concentrating on the ones that jump out at us in some way."

"I'm concentrating on all of them," Andrea said, and I had no doubt she was.

CHAPTER THIRTEEN

Andrea and I hadn't bothered to check Laszlo's and John's rental cars, assuming that there wouldn't be any evidence in them since the murders occurred in the hotel. At least that's what I assumed. In addition, three deputies had given them a thorough going-over, and then the sheriff had done the same. Still, I had no doubt Andrea would do some checking when they reached a rest stop on the way to Charleston.

"You're sure you don't want to go with us?" she asked as they were leaving. "We're planning lunch at The Outback."

"That's an enticing idea, but I'm not enthusiastic about riding down and back in one day. I'll stay here and keep an eye on things." Actually, it was more the idea of keeping an eye on things that persuaded me to stay.

They all smiled and nodded, and I couldn't help wondering whether they doubted my ability to play detective. Maybe I would show them, if I kept my eyes and ears open. It was a pleasant, sunny morning, and they waved and left with Stefan leading the way in Laszlo's car and Andrea bringing up the rear.

I went back into the hotel and took a deep breath of the coffee fragrance that was so enticing after coming in from the fresh air. Ivy was industriously working away at the computer, and I felt somewhat inadequate that I was a complete ignoramus in that field, while she seemed to be doing so well. Of course, she'd been practicing since they made her the desk clerk in January.

"Do you have any more weekenders checking in today, or did they all come yesterday?" I asked.

"We had three couples check in yesterday. Three couples, that is, in addition to the couple with the little boy that left. We have two more today, but they'll arrive late this afternoon."

"Is anyone in John Fuller's room?"

"No, I haven't put anyone in that wing. I'm trying to keep the guests away from the teenagers. I'm putting everyone upstairs. So far, they're all young and healthy folks and won't have a problem with the stairs."

"Andrea brought a sewing kit along, and I think I'll get it and mend that curtain in the Fuller room. That would give me something constructive to do while the others are gone. I'll get a cup of coffee first and take it with me. Do you want some?"

Ivy nodded toward her cup. "I still have plenty. Help yourself to the coffee and sweet rolls, too, if you want more."

"Well, maybe just one more."

I finished the roll and refilled my cup, and then went to our room to get Andrea's sewing kit. It occurred to me that there might be dried blood on the curtain, and I certainly didn't want to touch that. I hadn't noticed any when we all looked at the curtain lining before, but I'd check again when I got to the room, which was unlocked. They were still leaving the unoccupied rooms unlocked, and I couldn't see any reason why they shouldn't. There was nothing in them to steal.

The curtain lining looked clean; the long, thin slit in the fabric must have been made with something other than the knife that killed John Fuller. I threaded a needle with an off-white thread matching the lining and quickly stitched up the slit. Being a quilter, I've had lots of experience with a needle and thread. Quilting is something else Grandma Flynn taught me, and tried to teach Andrea. Somehow, it just didn't take with her.

I stood up and straightened the curtain. It would take a careful inspection by a guest to notice that the lining had been mended. I looked out toward Maggie's garden, colors glowing in the sunlight, and noticed that something was different. The garden didn't seem as big as when we previously saw it. I raised the window and looked some more. Something definitely was different.

I put the sewing kit back together as I'd found it and took it back to our room. Back in the lobby, I asked Ivy, "Have you noticed something different about Maggie's flower garden recently?"

"No, but I haven't been looking over that way as I go back and forth to the house. What's different about it?"

"It's smaller. I'm going out to check."

As I approached the flowers, I could see immediately what the difference was. The foxglove was gone. Someone had pulled it up. The area where it had been was neatly smoothed over, as if nothing had ever grown there. I stood there staring at the emptiness. I supposed Maggie and Stefan had gotten rid of the poisonous plant to prevent further use of it in someone's tea. I'd ask Maggie as soon as they got back. Or had the murderer hung it up somewhere to dry for use on more victims?

#

As I was walking back toward the front of the hotel, Juliet Gorsky drove up in her yellow Corvette convertible, her blonde hair blowing in the wind. "Good morning," she said as she got out. "I've been hiking again, and I'm starving. Would you like to go to lunch at the lodge?"

This would be a chance to get to know the woman better. "I'd love to, but I can't offer to drive. Andrea took the car."

"No problem. We'll take mine. Do you mind going with the top down?"

"Not at all. I'd enjoy it." I was hoping she'd say that, because I thought back as far as my teen years and couldn't remember riding in a convertible. Why not live dangerously—my hair was short.

"I need to go to my room first," she said.

We met in the lobby after I got my purse. By the time we reached the lodge, I was beginning to like my companion, in spite of the fact that athletic types like hikers make me feel inferior.

"Had you known Laszlo long?" I asked after we had placed our orders.

"Only for a few months. We got along very well, though, and he asked me if I'd like to come to the wedding. I had to come to the U.S. anyway, so I thought I might as well. He knew I'd enjoy the Canaan Valley, from what he'd read about it, and after researching it on the Internet, I was sure I would, too. I wasn't able to travel here with him, though, because of work commitments."

The waitress brought our food, but Juliet didn't start eating—she continued talking. "As you've probably figured out, I was hoping for a long-term relationship with him. We seemed perfect for each other, but it just wasn't to be. I hope to stay at the hotel till they find out who committed these terrible murders. I feel I owe it to Laszlo." She wiped away a tear and attacked her salad.

She certainly seemed innocent of murder, but as I'd told Andrea before, maybe she was the world's greatest actor. She was the only one, though, that had no apparent motive to kill either of the victims. I couldn't help smiling, thinking that we knew almost nothing about her, and she just might have a motive we didn't understand. She looked at me quizzically, and I fabricated, "I was just thinking how much I enjoyed riding in your car. Is it a rental?"

She smiled, too. "I bought it. I'm having it shipped home."

"And where is home?"

"I'm living in Paris at the moment."

We started eating and changed the subject to the view from the restaurant window and the many hiking opportunities in the valley.

#

Juliet went to her room for a nap, and I got my book and sat down by the fireplace to read. Right away I heard a door open down the hall, and I saw Nicole coming toward me with something in her hand. When she got closer, I could see it was a cup with a string hanging over the edge, as if it had a tea bag in it. Why was she carrying a cup through the lobby?

I smiled at her. "Having a cup of tea?"

She plopped down on the couch across from me. Her hair was messy and her eyes puffy, as if she'd just gotten up. "I'm just clearing up my sister's mess. I hate rooming with her. She's a slob!"

I was surprised she was talking to me, but I suppose she needed to vent to someone, and I was the only one around. I was also surprised Amalie was the slovenly one. "Where's the rest of your family?"

"They all went over to Dolly Sods. I didn't want to go. I wanted to sleep." She yawned.

She and David must have had another late night. "So you're cleaning up the room while they're gone."

"I have to, or it will drive me crazy. Yesterday, I found a plate with a half-eaten piece of cake under the bed. She makes tea and leaves cups all over the place. She has her stuff all over everything, so there's hardly a place to set a cup. I found this one on the shelf in the closet."

This news hit me like a spring breeze, clearing my mind. This must be the cup Laszlo drank from. Otherwise, why would Amalie have put it on the shelf in the closet? "I was just getting ready to wash my coffee cup, so I'll take care of that for you, and you can get back to cleaning."

She said "Thanks," yawned again, and got up and returned to her room.

I didn't know how to get in touch with the sheriff, but I dialed 911 on my cell phone and eventually got through to him. I explained about the cup, which I'd carefully put into a plastic bag, and he said he's be at the hotel shortly to pick it up. I put it in our room while I waited. I was hoping he'd come and go before the family got back. I didn't want Stefan to know I was collecting evidence against Amalie, since he can't believe his family members would murder anyone. As for me, I was now positive, once again, that Amalie was the guilty one.

I went to the porch to try out one of the Adirondack chairs. It was such a nice day, it was a pity to stay inside. I hadn't been sitting there long when a young lady drove up and parked under a tree at the edge of the parking lot. When she got out, I recognized her as Maggie's maid of honor and best friend, and I started searching my mind for her name. Just as she came up the steps to the porch, I remembered her first name. "Hello, Christina."

"Mrs. Williamson! How are you?"

"I'm fine. Are you looking for Maggie?"

"Yes. I just heard about Stefan's uncle. What a terrible thing to happen right after their wedding. I wanted to let them know how sorry I am."

"Maggie and Stefan have gone to Charleston to return the rental cars of the two men who were killed."

"There were two?"

"Yes, Mr. Novacek's partner was here also, and he was killed. Please have a seat. Do you mind if I ask you a question?" What I really wanted was to ask her several questions.

"Not at all. What is it?"

"Were you one of Maggie's friends who slept in the attic?"

"Yes, I was, and we had a blast. Most of us are good friends from the ski school. It was most disturbing to find out that while were having such a good time, someone was being murdered."

I lowered my voice. "Did you notice that anyone left the attic?"

"No, we were all too busy chatting and catching up on news. We hadn't been together since the end of ski season."

"So no one left at all?"

She thought about this for a moment. "Actually, the older woman left to go to the bathroom. I forgot about that."

"Did you notice how long she was gone?"

"I didn't give any thought to it, we were so busy taking. I think I had gone to sleep before she got back. I'm curious. Are they absolutely sure Mr. Novacek was murdered?"

"The autopsy results show that he was. Maybe it's best to keep our conversation confidential till the sheriff has an opportunity to sift through all the evidence."

Christina smiled. "I won't say a word. I'll be glad to talk with the sheriff if it's necessary."

I couldn't help thinking that any intrigue in the normally quiet Canaan Valley was exciting to young people, even if it involved murder. "I'll tell Stefan and Maggie you came by," I said.

Christina had been gone only a few minutes when the sheriff showed up. I went to my room and got the cup. I explained to Ward about the mysteriously disappearing foxglove, adding that Maggie and Stefan could have uprooted it, and also told him about my conversation with Christina. He simply nodded thoughtfully about all this, took the cup, and drove away.

At last, I was going to have clues to impart to Andrea that she knew nothing about. I couldn't wait. I sat down on the porch, and when my family arrived, Stefan was driving Andrea's car and she was in the backseat, talking on her cell phone. I knew without asking that she was talking to Ward

Sterling and he'd already told her everything that I was waiting breathlessly to divulge.

#

We hadn't seen Willard in a while, at least not when it was just the three of us, so we were hoping he'd be there when we drove up to the Canaan Lodge for breakfast. There was no sheriff's car in the parking area. But we had hardly been seated when he appeared. Sometimes I wonder if he cruises around looking for our car, hoping to impress us with what he knows.

He ordered toast and coffee. "I ate earlier at home. Hadley fixed me breakfast." He looked as if he'd had a wonderful night.

"Tell us about it, Willard." I had no doubt he would.

"Hadley and I are getting serious. She spends the night at my place now and then. Of course, her son's with her mother, so she has no worries about him being looked after."

"Where do you live?"

"I have a small house just off Highway 32. I inherited it from an aunt several years ago. It was a big surprise that she left it to me, but I've lived there ever since."

"And what does Hadley fix you for breakfast?" I wanted all the details.

"Well, this morning I had scrambled eggs and bacon. She even made biscuits. She won't fix eggs and bacon so often, because she says it's bad for my cholesterol. She looks after me." He was beaming by this time.

It was good to hear that Willard finally had a girlfriend who might work out for him. "She's very nice, and ambitious, too, going to school and working," I said.

The waitress brought our food, and Willard started slathering jam on his toast. "She has one more semester to go, and then she'll be getting a better job. We're talking about getting married."

"I hope we'll be invited to the wedding. We love an excuse to come to the valley. I just hope this wedding will come off with no disasters."

"We're going to count on it. You can be sure you'll be invited."

161

Andrea was taking this all in without saying a word. Then she spoke up. "How's the investigation going?"

He leaned toward us. "The blood on the knife was John Fuller's. No fingerprints have been found on anything, and we don't know where the knife came from. It's a hunting knife, and that's all we know."

"Who would have access to a hunting knife here," I asked.

"I suppose one of the guests could have brought it in their checked luggage."

"How about the memory card for the phone?"

"Henry got the glue off of it. He's waiting to put it in the phone till all the acetone has evaporated for sure. He doesn't want to mess up the phone by putting the card in prematurely. I think he's just nervous about inserting that card, thinking it might not work. I don't blame him."

"I keep thinking about the knife, and wondering why the killer left it in the room," Andrea said. "Why not take it with them and get rid of it somewhere where it wouldn't be found?"

"Maybe they were afraid to carry it down the hallway for fear someone would see them with it. And maybe they knew it couldn't be identified by anyone in this area. We've checked around and haven't found any have been sold lately."

I couldn't think of anything else to ask, and Andrea apparently couldn't either, so we concentrated on finishing breakfast. We told Willard goodbye in the parking lot and started back to the hotel. When we got there, Andrea went directly to Ivy at the desk. "Have you ever found the front door unlocked when you come to the lobby in the mornings?"

"Many times. By the time I get here, Asbury may have gone out to clean up the parking area, or Stefan may have gone outside. It's hard to tell who's coming and going around here."

"And if one of them finds the door unlocked, they may think someone else went out before them."

"Sure. And thought nothing of it. Like I say, security has been lax around here. We're tightening things up now. One of the deputies brought back the spare keys, and I put them in the safe. The old thing's as solid as a rock. I challenge anyone to break into that. I've got the combination memorized, too, so I tore up the paper Stefan gave me, just like he said to do."

Ivy's alright, I thought. She's a country woman through and through, but she knows what's important and how to take care of things. And she and Asbury are totally trustworthy. I had no doubt of that.

My thoughts were interrupted when the sheriff walked in. "Is Maggie here?"

"I suppose she's in the attic with Stefan," Andrea said.

"I'd like to talk to her. How do I get up there?"

"Is anything wrong?"

"I'll tell you on the way."

Andrea started for the attic stairs with Ward following, and I trailed along behind. No way was I going to miss this, if Maggie was involved. We went through the kitchen, into the laundry room, and Andrea opened the door to the attic stairs.

The sheriff led the way. "Henry put the memory card in the phone, and it worked. We discovered that Laszlo called a local number at eleven the night he was killed. Someone from the same number called him back at midnight. Henry's checking now to see who that number belongs to."

"Why the urgency to see Maggie?" I asked.

"I can't say she's in danger for sure, but we're just trying to be cautious."

"You're thinking the number belongs to Eva," Andrea said.

"We can't think of anyone else local he'd be calling at that time of night."

My legs were beginning to feel as if they might not hold me up. Could Eva be a possible danger to Maggie? Somehow, it didn't make sense.

Ward's phone rang as we reached the top. "Yes? Okay, thanks." He hung up. "The number was Eva's."

We could see Stefan and David at the far end of the attic, and the sheriff went that way. "Where's Maggie?" he asked when we reached them.

Stefan put down his hammer. "She's gone to Elkins. Is there a problem?"

"Did she go alone?"

"No, she went with Eva. As you probably know, they haven't gotten along so well, and she thought it might be an opportunity for reconciliation. Eva asked her to go to the mall."

Ward turned and headed for the stairs. Stefan started after him, with Andrea and me right behind. "What's going on?" Stefan demanded.

"Andrea can explain. I have to go." By this time we were at the bottom of the stairs, and he rushed out through the laundry room and kitchen and toward the front door.

"I'm going with you," Stefan said, and jumped into the front seat of the patrol car.

"I am too," Andrea said as Ward started the engine.

I didn't take time to say anything but ran around the car and jumped in the other side. I managed to close the door just as we screeched out of the parking lot. Andrea and I buckled up.

"Somebody explain this to me," Stefan said.

"Explain, Andrea. I'm too busy driving." But instead of just driving, he dialed his cell phone and asked the person on the other line to send officers to the mall. The officers should check inside for a couple of young women, a blonde and a redhead, and keep an eye on them.

Meanwhile, Andrea started explaining to Stefan. "I discovered earlier today that Eva's mother was involved in the same venture where your relatives lost money. Then later, Henry with the sheriff's office was able to get Laszlo's phone card to work. It showed that he called Eva at eleven on the night of his death, and she called him back at midnight. As you can see, things are beginning to add up. Ward is concerned that she may have plans to harm Maggie."

"Impossible! Why would she want to harm Maggie?"

"Everyone in the valley knows she's madly in love with you. Do I have to say more? She's obsessed with you."

"That doesn't mean she'd try to kill Maggie."

"If the clues are pointing in the right direction, and she's already killed two people, then it's possible."

No one said anything for a while, and I was back to concentrating on the road. Ward was zooming around curves even faster than Andrea usually does. Something else the two of them have in common. I was trying to concentrate on the highway and Ward's driving so I wouldn't be so concerned about Maggie. Whatever possessed her to go off to Elkins with Eva?

I asked Stefan just that. He said, "I don't think she would have gone, except that she's almost out of her favorite perfume—something from Estee Lauder. She buys it in Charleston, but she thought she might be able to get it at the Tygart Valley Mall. She knows I love for her to use it, because I love it too. It's just her. If anything happens to her because she's trying to please me, I'll never forgive myself."

"We don't know yet that Eva killed anyone," Andrea said. "And even if she did, we don't know she's thinking of harming Maggie."

No one could think of anything else to say. We all were concentrating on getting there. We finally hit Highway 33, and the road straightened out and became wider. Now Ward really put on the speed, and we were soon entering Elkins. We arrived at the mall shortly, and Ward started driving through the parking area, looking for Eva's car. Finally, Stefan spotted it, and it was empty. Two empty police cruisers were parked near the mall entrance.

Ward started down a lane toward the main mall entrance, and ahead of us we saw Maggie and Eva. "See, they're just going shopping. Nothing to worry about," Stefan said. "On the other hand, I think I'll go in and make up something about Maggie being urgently needed at home. She can ride back with us."

At that moment a man emerged from between two parked cars and walked toward the women. He was so intent on approaching them that he didn't notice the patrol car coming his way. *Odd that he's wearing a jacket on such a warm day*, I thought. Then his hand came out from under the jacket, and he was holding a gun. "Maggie! Look out!" I screamed, but she didn't hear me.

It didn't matter, because Ward swerved the car and took the man's legs out from under him. I realized I was still screaming, and Andrea grabbed my arm and shook me. The gun went flying, and Eva ran for it. She picked it up and pointed it at Maggie. Stefan jumped out of the car and ran toward her. She dropped the gun. She grabbed Maggie by the hair and slammed her to the pavement. "I hate you," she

165

screamed over and over. Stefan grabbed her arms and held them behind her, and Ward immediately had handcuffs in place.

A dozen people must have called the police, because city officers, an ambulance, and Randolph County deputies came pouring onto the scene. Two policemen came from the mall and joined the others. I felt as if I were dreaming as someone put Eva into a police car. EMS technicians loaded up the man who originally had the gun; someone was now picking it up and putting it into a plastic bag.

We were there for what seemed like hours, giving statements and waiting while others gave statements. We gave addresses, home phone numbers, cell phone numbers, and the Alpenhof address and phone number. I was expecting them to ask my bra size next. I finally collapsed into Ward's car when I figured they were through with me. Maggie was already there rubbing her head where Eva slammed her to the ground. We hugged each other and started sobbing.

After another eternity, Ward, Andrea, and Stefan came. We had managed to wipe away the tears by then, and were feeling somewhat giddy—or maybe hysterical would be a better word. Stefan got in the back beside Maggie and put his arm around her. Andrea sat in front with Ward. We started for home.

"She wanted to get rid of me so she could have you," Maggie said.

Stefan laughed and hugged her tighter. "It never would have worked. Can you see Eva putting up Sheetrock?"

EPILOGUE

The man with two broken legs told everything he knew. In the hospital with casts, bruises, and bandages, a policeman standing watch at his door, and an interviewer from the prosecutor's office at his bedside, he was ready to make a deal. He had met Eva in a bar in Elkins, and after seeing her there several times and chatting with her, she asked him to join her in a booth. She bought him drinks. Then she offered him two thousand dollars to shoot Maggie in the chest, as many times as it took.

He was to steal Maggie's purse, and Eva would run screaming toward the mall. He should go to Eva's car, get in, and hide in the backseat. She would circle back around and join him, and then drive him to safety. She'd have his money in the car. The prosecutor explained to him that Eva's car was locked, and no money was found in it.

Eva's in the Randolph County Jail with bond set so high she'll never make it. Her finances are in a shambles. Her husband came from Germany to clear out the rent house. He's been paying the rent and utilities there, feeling sorry for Eva in spite of himself. He identified the hunting knife as one he inherited from his grandfather, who used to hunt in the Black Forest. He left it in the house when he returned to Germany, thinking he'd come back to the valley, but he decided on a divorce while he was away. The knife is a family heirloom, and Ward promised it will be returned to him eventually. He has no interest in bailing Eva out of jail. He's going back to Germany as fast as he can to finalize the divorce.

Ward and his deputies are busy building a case so that Eva can be charged with the two murders, as well as the attempted murder of Maggie. They found a freshly-dug spot of earth in Eva's backyard, and when they investigated, a teabag was found there. It's being analyzed now. The foxglove from Maggie's garden was drying in a spare bedroom, and I couldn't help wondering just how many more of us she intended to poison.

Ward suggested that we go to the Cheat River Inn for dinner a couple of days after the Elkins incident. Word spread somehow, as it always does in the Canaan Valley, and pretty soon everyone wanted to go with us. All of Stefan's relatives, the sisters, David and Nicole, and even Willard and Hadley showed up, looking like a pair of lovebirds. We practically filled the place, and everyone was in a jolly mood, happy that it hadn't been a family member who was guilty of murder.

Franz insisted on paying the entire bill and tip, and no one argued. We were all too emotionally drained to put up an argument about anything. When we left, I couldn't help noticing that Ward had his arm around Andrea's shoulders. I heard him tell her he'd come down to Pine Summit for a weekend soon. Funny, but they didn't look like a pair of lovebirds at all. They looked like a couple of stiffly formal older folks who weren't really comfortable with any public display of affection.

The next morning, most everyone was packing up for the drive back to Charleston. They'd spend the night there and fly out the next day. Maggie, Stefan, Andrea and I said goodbye to them in the parking lot with lots of hugs and cheek kisses. I was getting into the swing of that myself. David was there, too, hanging around Nicole and looking uncomfortable, as if he didn't know how to tell her goodbye. Nicole solved the problem by grabbing him and giving him a big smooch on the mouth. Andrea and I planned to stay for a couple more days. Since Maggie's life had been threatened, we weren't quite ready to leave her yet.

One member of the European group wasn't going, though, and Andrea and I were delighted. Maggie and Stefan invited Agnes to stay with them indefinitely. Maggie normally works the desk in the evenings, but they had planned to replace her when they got married. They offered Agnes the job, without pay until they can get her a green card, whatever that is. She'll stay in Maggie's room till Eva's husband finishes clearing out the rent house, and then she'll move in there. It's within easy walking distance of the Alpenhof.

Agnes is sweet, intelligent, and has such a beautiful, subtle accent, she'll be great on the registration desk. And my guess is that she's going to enjoy having the Atlantic Ocean between her and Claudia. She's developed a happy glow already.

She sat down with us in the kitchen after everyone left, and Andrea started another pot of coffee. We'd had lots of sweet rolls and Danish earlier with the travelers, and there were a few pastries left. Ivy called Asbury to come and cover the desk for a while, and she joined us. She obviously wanted to get to know Agnes better, since they'd both be working the desk. Then, just like clockwork, Willard showed up. He helped himself to coffee and a Danish and sat down with us.

"Hadley and I are thinking about October," he told me.

Everyone's ears perked up. "Are you and Hadley . . .? Ivy started to ask.

"We're seriously considering getting married. We think October would be the perfect time."

It's the loveliest time in West Virginia, when the hardwoods are at their most showy. I love a trip to the Canaan Valley in October. "Just let us know. We'll be here."

Agnes went upstairs to move her few belongings into Maggie's room, and Willard went back to work. Then Andrea left to find her book for a morning of reading. Ivy and I were alone and were having a second cup of coffee. "What do you make of the fact that there was a murder on the night of the full moon, and that a murderer was caught in the dark of the moon?" I asked. "According to what we know about moon signs, it should have been the other way around."

"Sometimes things are too complicated for us to understand. I don't know how else to explain it." However she explained it, I knew that neither Ivy nor I would ever lose our confidence in living life according to the signs of the moon.

ABOUT THE AUTHOR

Helen Haught Fanick's short stories have appeared in Women's Household, Midnight Zoo, Vermont Ink, and in various anthologies and e-zines. Her articles and photos have been published in Texas Observer, Stepping Stones, and other publications. Her poem, Leaf Fall, appeared in Nature's Gifts, an anthology published by Vanilla Heart Publishing to benefit The Nature Conservancy. She has won several local and state awards, and two national awards in the Writer's Digest Competition. She is a graduate of The University of Texas at San Antonio with a degree in English and lives in San Antonio with her husband.

Her novel *Moon Signs,* Book I of the Moon Mystery Series, was previously published with Create Space and is also available at www.amazon.com for Kindle users. Her upcoming novel, *Saving Susie,* will be published soon in both paperback and ebook form. Continue reading for an excerpt from *Saving Susie.*

SAVING SUSIE
By
Helen Haught Fanick

CHAPTER ONE

My son Jason and I had finished dinner and were still at the table, having coffee, and talking about a matter that had been coming up all too frequently lately. Jason wanted to drop out of college after his junior year and go to work full-time in the print shop I owned in downtown San Gabriel. I wanted him to finish his business degree and continue to work part-time until graduation.

Jason was a lot like his father—the same light brown hair, gray eyes, and the same impulsiveness. I tried to get him to give some logical thought to his decisions, but like most twenty-year-olds, he didn't want to listen to his mother. Our discussions about his future usually ended in a stalemate; this one ended when the police rang our doorbell.

I looked through the peephole and saw buttons and a silver badge on an expanse of blue. I stepped back and blinked, taking a second to grasp the situation.

"Who is it, Mom?" Jason asked.

"It's the police." My voice was quavering.

"Why would they be here?"

I could tell by the tone of his voice that he knew without asking but was hoping it wasn't so. After all, if you're breaking only one law in your household, it's logical to assume the police are at your door for that reason. "What else could it be? They're after Susie."

We had thought we didn't have a problem when the City of San Gabriel, Texas, passed a law banning pit bull terriers within city limits. The city's action was taken after a couple of attacks last year by vicious dogs with irresponsible, anti-social owners. But Susie was eleven years old and had never bitten anyone. If I opened the door, she'd be wagging her entire body, hoping to be petted, as she did every time someone rang the bell. Most callers jumped back in terror but quickly were won over by her pleading look when I told them she wouldn't bite.

She was an inside dog who liked to sniff around in the small fenced garden behind our town house. We took her walking late in the evening, when the streets were deserted, or nearly deserted. Most of our neighbors knew Susie and made a fuss over her when they saw her. I wondered how the police knew about her.

My thoughts flitted to the scowling woman I ran into on our walk two nights ago. She had picked up her poodle and crossed the street when she saw us coming in spite of the fact that Susie was wagging her tail and straining at her leash, hoping to play. Had the woman seen me enter our town house and called the police with our address?

We had thought we could keep Susie with us until we found a suitable place for her. Now she sat in front of the door, her tail wagging in a frenzy of joy at hearing the doorbell ring a second time. She tipped her head to one side, eager to greet our visitor. I was thankful she didn't bark.

My heart was thumping as I struggled to decide whether to hide Susie upstairs or to get her out of the house. The doorbell rang a third time.

Jason dragged her away from the door. "You stall them. I'll get her out the back way."

"No, you have that accounting test tomorrow to study for," I whispered. "I'll take her through the back and into the car. Keep them here till I get away."

"Dad's been promising to find a place for her ever since they passed the pit bull law. I'll call him and . . ."

"I'll call him. Just stall the police till we get out of here." I grabbed my keys from the rack by the door and snatched my purse from the counter. I put my fingers under Susie's collar and led her toward the door to the garage.

The doorbell rang for a fourth time, and I heard Jason shout, "Just a minute!"

I closed the door softly between the kitchen and garage, then unlocked the car and let Susie into the back. "Lie down," I whispered, and she curled up on the seat and put her head down.

173

I raised the garage door, then stepped outside and looked around. A police car was parked behind the town house next to ours, and an officer was sitting in it. Thank God all these town houses look alike, I thought. I got into the car and hissed at Susie, "Lie down! Stay!" even though she hadn't moved since my previous command. I backed out and pressed the button to close the garage door.

I checked the street in both directions. The policeman glanced at me and picked up his radio. He said something and listened for a moment, then put the radio down. My heart rate had slowed a little, but now it accelerated. I looked up and down the street and pulled out slowly. The officer looked back toward the seat beside him as if he were doing paperwork.

I drove down the street and turned at the first corner. My rearview mirror told me I wasn't being followed. I made several more turns getting out of the neighborhood, then entered the expressway and went across town. I couldn't help worrying about Susie all the way, wondering what my next move should be. I couldn't imagine giving her up, but it was obvious we could no longer ignore the law.

Jason and I had been trying to come up with a plan we could live with ever since the ordinance had been passed. His father had promised to help him find a home for Susie in the country, and I had maintained my usual silent skepticism about how much help he would be.

We'd been in no great hurry to find a solution. Susie was the friendliest dog in town. We assumed, erroneously it seemed, that the police wouldn't know about her and that our neighbors, knowing how friendly she was, wouldn't turn us in. Maybe they hadn't, but someone had. The lady with the poodle must have called them.

I got off the expressway and stopped at a supermarket, wishing I had taken time to grab my cell phone, which I had plugged into the charger in the bedroom as soon as I got home. I took the change from my coin purse and went to a pay phone attached to the brick front of the store. I would have to call Randall to see whether he had made any progress in solving the problem of Susie. My only alternative was to drive five hundred miles across Texas to Aunt Catherine's in El Paso to see whether she could put us up while I found a home for

Susie. Unfortunately, she hated dogs. I've never been sure she liked me very much, either, even though I lived with her for several years when I was young.

I lifted the receiver and dropped coins into the slot, then dialed the number and waited as it rang seventeen times. Why didn't the answering machine come on? Did he have call waiting? My ex never had been there when I needed him. Why should this evening be any different? Just as I started to hang up, I heard a click. I slammed the receiver back against my ear and said, "Hello!"

"Hello. Denise?"

"Yes. I need help. I'm calling about Susie."

"What happened?"

"The police came tonight. I'm pretty sure they were looking for her." My voice was trembling, and I couldn't say any more. A tear trickled from under the lashes of my right eye.

"Jesus! Where are you now? Where's Susie?" He sounded concerned. Possibly a good sign.

I found a tissue in my pocket and wiped away the tear, then took a moment to get my voice under control. "I'm at some supermarket on the north side. Susie's in the car. I got her out through the garage."

"What are you going to do?"

Fury began to replace distress as my dominant emotion. "The question is, what are you going to do? You're the one who bought Susie in the first place, but you never have taken any responsibility for her."

"We were married then. You agreed to it when I bought her." His voice was cold and hushed; someone must be at the apartment with him.

"Okay, let's not argue about it. You've been telling Jason for weeks you'd help him find a place for her. Do you know anyone at all who could take her? Maybe just a temporary arrangement till we can work out something else?"

"Possibly. I can check on it. Can you call me back in a couple of hours?"

"No, I can't call you back in a couple of hours. I'm at a strange supermarket at a pay phone. I need to know whether you can find a solution before I decide what I have to do tonight."

"Oh, hell. Give me the number there. I'll call you back later."

"When?"

"In an hour or so."

"Why should it take so long? If you can get in touch with someone, you should be able to call in fifteen minutes. And if you can't, call me back in fifteen minutes and tell me you can't."

"Denise, I wish I had a recording of this conversation. You used to wonder why our marriage broke up. Maybe if you could hear yourself, you'd understand."

"What do you mean?" I was near tears again.

"You're so exacting."

There were a lot of retorts I could have made, but I calmly gave him the number on the pay phone and told him if I didn't hear from him in fifteen minutes, I'd bring Susie over and leave her tied to his doorknob.

I got back into the car, reached over the seat, and scratched her ears. "I didn't mean it, Susie," I muttered. For weeks I had been avoiding serious consideration of the idea that we'd have to give Susie to someone else. Now I would have to face that painful fact, keep it together, and find a solution.

I glanced at my wrist. My watch was on the dresser at home where I always put it, with the band stretched out parallel to my jewelry box. The clock in the car said it was seven-thirty. It had only been a couple of minutes since I hung up the phone. I'd give Randall until a quarter to eight, and then what, if he didn't call?

Worry about that fifteen minutes from now, I told myself. For the moment, just think about—what? The police. Running from the police was an experience I had never imagined, not even in my most extreme fantasies. Yet somewhere beneath the fear for Susie and the frustration of being trapped by an unjust law, a tiny grain of something like excitement was beginning to irritate the surface of my orderly life.

I'd have to dig it out and examine it when things returned to normal. Obviously such an irritant couldn't be expected to develop into a pearl if left alone. A festering sore would be the most likely outcome. In the meantime, a tall young man with really strange hair walked up to the pay phone, put money into it, and dialed a number at seventeen till eight.

I slammed my fist into the seat beside me. If I had been thinking clearly, I would have pretended to be talking on the phone until Randall called back. I got out of the car and stood beside it. The young man with the enormously spiked hair had a large silver chain around his waist. I cleared my throat, and he turned his head, gave me a cold stare, and kept on talking.

I retreated into the car and slammed the door. While I drummed my fingers against the steering wheel, the clock changed to fourteen till eight. Randall was trying to get through and getting a busy signal. Why hadn't I just told him I'd call him back? Too much sudden stress had muddled my thinking.

My stomach tightened into a hard lump, and I closed my eyes and breathed deeply, concentrating on relaxing everything from my toes to my scalp. The technique had worked in my stress relief class; now it didn't seem to help.

Maybe if I got out of the car with Susie, it would scare the kid at the phone and he would just hang up and go away. But could I take a chance on calling that much attention to us? A few cars were passing on the street behind me, and an occasional customer came out of the store pushing a cart, but otherwise everything was quiet. If I waited too long, Randall probably would take whoever he was with out to dinner and forget all about Susie and me.

I got out and opened the back door for Susie. We edged as close to the young man as we could while still keeping Susie hidden behind the fender. "Sit," I told her, in order to keep her wagging tail from showing.

The young man turned, and his face lit up when he saw her. "Hello, girl," he said as he squatted down and reached out to pat her head. "No, there's a pit bull here, a really neat one. Yeah, she's real heavy-set. She's tan with white feet, and her muzzle's black. It has some gray in it. She must be getting old." As he continued to stroke Susie's head and scratch her cropped ears, I could see they were two kindred souls in complete and blissful rapport with each other. So much for scaring him away.

I cleared my throat. "Excuse me, but I'm expecting a call on this phone."

"Lady, you can't tie up a pay phone because you're expecting a call. Get serious." He turned his attention back to Susie and continued to talk alternately to her and to the person on the other end of the line. "No, I'm talking to the owner. A real babe. I'm squatting down here patting the dog, and I have a great view of a terrific pair of legs. About thirty-five, I'd say."

I was irritated rather than flattered by his remarks, but I managed to keep my voice pleasantly in control. "I really need you to give up this phone."

He stood up. "You'd better get this dog out of here. They outlawed them here, you know."

"I know. That's what the phone call I'm expecting is about. I'm trying to arrange a way to get her out of San Gabriel."

"Why didn't you say so? Hey, I'll call you back later." He hung up the receiver. "You'd better get her back in the car." He disappeared into the store.

The phone rang just as I was shutting Susie into the back seat. I rushed to the receiver. "Hello!"

"Denise?"

"Yes." Shaking all over, I leaned against the building.

"Who in the devil was tying up the line? I've been trying to get through for ten minutes."

"Some kid, talking to a friend. I couldn't get him to give up the phone. Did you find out anything?"

"I think I have something worked out."

"You think?"

"Well, I do have something worked out. There's a guy that owes me a favor. He has an airplane, and he's going to fly you to Mexico."

"Mexico? Why on earth to Mexico?"

"There are some people down there who want to take Susie. Their name is Gutierrez, and they have a large estate on the Yucatan Peninsula. They have a landing strip and everything. It'll be a good place for her."

"I don't know what to say. We'd never be able to see her down there. Jason's going to be heartbroken."

"Stop and think, Denise. Isn't it better to make a clean break? If you see her later on, she'd always be wanting to go home with you. This way she can adjust to a new family, and you and Jason can get on with your lives."

I was fighting back tears again, and I took a deep breath to steady my voice. It was time to concentrate on the plan rather than on my feelings. "Do these people know we're coming?"

"I just called them. They're expecting you. And I called Steve Wingfield, the pilot. He's going to meet you tomorrow morning. There are several hangars along the east side of Bingham Field. He's in number thirteen. He wants you to come out there by six-thirty. Park in that area just beside the hangars."

"I'm still not sure about this. Is this man a good pilot?"

"Sure. He's been flying for years. And the way I see it, Denise, there's no alternative. I haven't been able to find anyone else who would take her. We discussed your Aunt Catherine, but you know she hates dogs. Would she be willing to take you both in while you find a home for Susie?"

"Probably not."

"Denise, be at Wingfield's hangar at six-thirty in the morning. Believe me, this is for the best. I have to go now. I'm late for an appointment. I'd appreciate it if you would reimburse me for that call to Mexico. Things have been tight lately. I have to hang up now. Call me when you get back." I heard a click and then a dial tone.

Made in the USA
Columbia, SC
16 March 2018